DRAGON THIRST

Legends

T.B. PHILLIPS

Dragon Thirst: Legends

Published by Andalon Press
Copyright © 2023 by T.B. Phillips

Cover design by Lynnette Bonner of Indie Cover Design, images ©
    stock.adobe.com, File: # 521064390 – dragon scales
    stock.adobe.com, File: # 606626360 – dragon eye
    depositphotos.com, File: # 40346871_L – fire
    stock.adobe.com, File: # 484733654 – dragon clipart
    stock.adobe.com, File: # 186849468 – dragon crest
Book interior design by Stewart Design, https://StewartDesign.studio

ISBN 978-1-961674-04-2

This is a work of fiction. Names, characters, places, and incidents are a product of the author's imagination. Locales and public names are sometimes used for atmospheric purposes. Any resemblance to actual people, living or dead, or to businesses, companies, events, institutions, or locales is completely coincidental.

Books by T.B. Phillips

Dragon Thirst
Legends (September 2023)
Mythos (September 2023)

Andalon Saga

Andalon Origins
Andalon Project (April 2022)
Andalon Paradox (April 2023)
Andalon Prophecies (Expected Winter 2023)

Dreamers of Andalon
Andalon Awakens (June 2019)
Andalon Arises (July 2020)
Andalon Attacks (December 2020)

Children of Andalon
Andalon Legacy (September 2022)

Corrupted Realms
Orphan Knight (July 2023)
Wailing Tempest (May 2021)
Howling Shadow (September 2021)

Chilling Tales
Ferryman (October 2022)

Corrupted Realms
Orphan Knight (July 2023)
Wailing Tempest (April 2021)
Howling Shadow (September 2021)

Dragon Thirst: Legends

In the beginning the world belonged to mankind—fledgling and barely emerged from wilderness. The arrival of divine messengers, harbingers sent to forge a world in which humans would thrive, nearly sped their downfall instead. Arriving with grace but blinded by arrogance, the divine blazed a prosperous path benefiting themselves. But soon these Keryx found their charges alluring, the simplistic beauty of human form fanned insatiable desire.

The resulting offspring, known as Titans or Nephilim, are recounted separately by every culture's legends. They ruled over earth and treated mankind as simple animals. Man wrote these creatures into their story as gods—today they live among us as legends.

This is the story of those ancient and divine bloodlines, how they existed alongside simple humans, steering their lives while committed to the total destruction of rivals. It tells of variants who emerged as mythological heroes and foes.

The bloodlines of these Keryx war to this day...

Choose your form...

A pair of eyes blinked open finding only darkness. Aching muscles suggested the owner of these eyes had spent too long in fetal curl. He felt around the cramped surroundings, caged by sticky walls that squeezed tightly. The smoothness of the barrier seemed foreign, its substance a mystery, neither ridged like wooden boards nor pitted as stone would have been. This prison seemed different, so much so the prisoner panicked.

His nails had grown long during slumber but were not brittle. He scraped them against a sticky palm, pressing and testing their strength. They felt sharper somehow, ridged for the task. Shifting his body the best he could, he first scratched then clawed, finally chipping away at the layer between him and freedom.

Lightheadedness slowly crept in, resembling panic, and the man soon realized he lacked air. Stifling suffocation fueled him to chip faster at the prison wall. Prison? This now felt more like a tomb.

His nails throbbed from his efforts so he ceased chipping. Instead he punched, swinging his arm the best he could while curled so tightly. Tap. Tap. Tap. The effort proved futile but he refused to stop. He *had* to get free or he would die from lack of air. With one final push his hand felt the wall give just enough. Tiny cracks formed where his energy had focused.

His nails went to work at once, tearing and ripping, trying to pry these cracks wider. Eventually, he managed to break away a single section no bigger than his palm. Pressing an eye against the opening he stared out, finding more darkness waiting outside.

He breathed stale air through the tiny hole and rested, exhausted by the effort but no less deterred. He *would* free himself. After a few minutes he tried again, this time finding the cracks easier to break away. Slowly, the opening grew. Eventually, the man slipped free.

His strength fully expended, he lay on cold stone, sticky, naked, and coated with moisture. He breathed slowly with lungs eager for air. Sleep took over...

"Wake up!" a woman's voice commanded.

He stirred but found it difficult to move. Every muscle hurt.

"I know you've awakened early," the woman said, "but danger comes, and you won't be able to defend yourself."

The man stretched, his muscles aching from cramps. He expected weakness. *How long have I been trapped?* he wondered. But somehow his muscles had not atrophied. He rolled to his belly and tried to get onto all fours. His hands were coated with that residue and caused him to slip. His face landed hard against the stone. He blinked his eyes, unseeing in the blackness. He tried to speak, but no words came.

"Easy now," the woman's voice cautioned, tenderly but not without authority. "You've only just awakened, and your body has changed. It moves differently than it did before. Go slowly and let it adjust."

He put one hand against the ground followed by the other, wiping his palms before getting onto his knees. To his surprise his hips and core muscles held him upright. He drew in a deep breath before trying to stand.

"But don't go too slowly," the voice urged. "We cannot fight so many and must flee."

"Who..." his voice tested the air around him while his mind struggled for words. "Who are you?" he asked.

"Who I am doesn't matter. Not yet. What matters is who *you* are. Do you remember anything at all?"

Dragons. The word echoed in his mind, followed by another. *Vampires.*

"What of the war?" the woman pressed. "Do you remember why you transformed?"

Images fluttered around, disorganized thoughts popping up as memories or imaginations. He had no way to distinguish which. Slowly, some of these came into focus.

"I... I don't even know who *I* am," the man whispered.

"That's normal," the woman promised. "When I awakened, I felt that way for several hours, with some memories not returning for weeks after. Even now, *years* later, I am still discovering the knowledge with which we were entrusted."

"Who are *you*?" the man weakly demanded.

"You will have to discover that in time, along with your own memories. Anything I tell you now may confuse facts as you once knew them. But I promise you will know all this and more very soon. Reach to your right," she told him, "and you will find a bucket of water and rags. Drink from it first, then use the rest to cleanse your body of the yolk."

Yolk? Had his prison been an egg?

The idea felt so foreign but seemed to fit with the images he had imagined. Picking up the bucket, he drank deeply, then set it down and picked up the rags. He wished for light so that he could see his body as he wiped it down.

It *did* feel different than he expected. His muscles, body hair, all of him seemed to belong to someone else. Even his thoughts belonged to someone else.

"After you are clean, feel to your left and find the clothing I laid out for you. It may seem strange at first but put it on the best you can. We can adjust it later."

He put down the rags and felt around the stone to his left. Several folded garments were placed in a pile, and he put them on in the order he found them, touching the openings and guessing to which part of his body they belonged. The last items he found was a pair of leather boots. The smell brought forth new images. He let these cycle through, then pulled on the footwear.

"I'm sorry we have to move so soon before you're ready," the voice said with a hint of sincerity, "but a battle rages at the entrance to this cave. We cannot leave that way, but I know of another."

The man felt two soft hands grab his own and allowed the stranger to pull him onto his feet. She helped steady him, then pressed an object into his hand.

He felt the leather sheath, smooth and soft, and squeezed the hard object within. It felt like a blade and drew it slowly across his finger to feel the edge. It was a mistake given the soft state his skin was in, and a tiny trickle of blood warmed the coolness of his hand.

"Careful!" the woman hissed. "Tie it to your waist and let's be gone."

His hands fumbled in the blackness, cramped and bruised from breaking out of his prison. *I hatched out of an egg,* he thought, his mind filling with an image of row after row of eggs lining the walls of some distant cavern. This, he was certain, was also a memory. As soon has he had tied the knot, the woman grabbed his hand and led him away.

"Don't worry," she said, pulling him into a passage. "Your eyes will recover, so will your mind, faster even. By the time we reach the surface you will see clearly."

At her words, he realized the darkness clouding his vision was actual blindness. He felt a surge of panic jolt his heart. It beat faster. He was afraid, then, that the woman's voice would lead him away and then leave him lost and alone in these caverns. Yet, at the same time, her voice had a familiarity. He felt both fear and trust for this woman, whoever she may be.

The tunnel she led him through grew lower. Soon she told him to duck. He found himself crawling on his hands and knees through narrow passages, following her voice. Despite his worries she never left him and eventually led him to a cool breeze and the soft sounds of nature.

Together, the pair approached the surface. In the distance a soft glow had formed in front of his eyes, suggesting moonlight waited ahead. As promised, his eyesight gradually strengthened and he soon made out the woman who led him. She was beautiful, in her late twenties with long black hair and pale skin. Her eyes, he noticed, were a fierce crimson and seemed oddly wrong. For some reason he had expected them to be blue. When they reached the opening, she turned with a sad look as if holding a dark secret, she yearned to tell it. She managed a brief smile filled with worry.

"We're almost there," she said as the passage grew enough they could once more walk upright. "Keep your blade ready just in case."

"Just in case of what?" he asked, hoping the visions flashing in his mind were not the reason she feared. These foul creatures were hideous, gaunt with oversized bones and skin stretched as if it were grey leather drying on a rack. They grinned at him with pointed fangs that cut their lips, leaving tiny trails of blood along their chins.

"You'll know them when you see them," she said.

"I think I do somehow, I just don't know the name for them," he admitted. Then a word reached his mind, bringing with it vile repulsion. "Is it *voltur*?" he asked.

"Very good," the woman said proudly. This time her smile lingered. "It won't be long until you fully remember your other form."

Other form? So, he had not just been hatched, not as an infant it would seem. Whatever he had hatched from was more like a butterfly's cocoon instead. "Is that what I just did? I emerged from a cocoon?"

"In a way."

"What am I then?" he asked. He felt like a man.

"You are what you chose," she replied curtly, "and I won't explain any more until you remember the rest on your own."

He fell silent, considering her words. No matter how hard he tried to make himself, the memories remained hidden from that remembrance. He thought instead of the voltur, visualizing them sleeping with arms crossed and eyes closed. One by one he drew a strange blade, stabbing them in the chest and staring into the swirling pools of blood which were their eyes.

Another thought made itself clear, a vision of a larger, more humanoid version of the creatures. These had long leathery wings, the same fangs, and, most disturbingly, the same bloody orbs for eyes. "Vampure," he said suddenly.

"Yes, those too," she agreed.

A strange feeling overtook him, a sense of déjà vu more than a vision or a memory. He *felt* it more than he saw or thought it, and suddenly exclaimed, "There's one close by."

"What?" The woman spun to look at him. "Why did you say that?"

"I don't know, I just... I *feel* a presence that my mind faintly remembers."

"Well, you're wrong," she quickly snapped.

Finally, she had answered one of his questions, even if she hadn't meant to give herself away. "So, we *can* feel them?" he asked. "I'm not imagining this feeling?"

"Of course not. What you're feeling must be confusion in your mind, memories mixing with imagination as the visions settle themselves out."

"So *you* can't feel them?"

"Don't be ridiculous. As great an ability that would be, no. We can't *feel* vampure any more than they can *sense* us." The irritation in her voice had grown. Whoever she was, this woman lacked patience and seemed full of resentment.

"Well, I swear I can," the man pressed. And he could, as a nagging sensation he couldn't shake off. Her silence said enough, and he dropped the issue, stepping out from the cave into the cool night. Taking in a deep breath, he let the clean air fill his lungs, replacing the mustiness that reminded him now of imprisonment. He was free, thanks to this woman's help, free to walk the surface. *But where?* he wondered. Nothing except the moonlight seemed familiar.

The land stretched out for many miles in all directions, mostly flat, but rugged and rocky. Off in the west and south, the land folded and rose into soft hills that seemed chiseled by angry giants. Most surprisingly, there were no snowcapped mountains anywhere.

"It's odd," the man said. "This place is different than any vision I've seen since awakening. It's like I emerged on a different planet."

"Yes," the woman agreed. "I thought so too when I stepped outside."

"You hatched like I did?"

"I did, but there was no one to help me. I crawled out naked, terrified, and had to wander the caves alone until I found help."

"Why?" the man asked. "Why me? Why come back to help me, and how did you know I would hatch?"

"Awakened" she corrected. "Stop saying *hatch* like you were just born."

"Okay, how did you know I would awaken when I did?"

"You weren't supposed to, not yet. But I needed your help and so I hurried you along."

"Why? What's so dire that you woke me? Was it those creatures I imagined? Those voltur?"

"Yes, them *and* the vampure."

"What are they?"

"Look, I awakened you early, but I can't tell you anything about your past. You have to figure the details out on your own, or what I say will taint the truth you gained during transformation."

The man considered this. So far he trusted the woman, but she seemed to be in such a hurry. He looked around. There were no voltur, none of the vampure either. Only miles of open land and a soft glow on the distant horizon. "What's that?" he asked. "Is something burning in that direction?"

"No, it's a city."

That made no sense, not with such a bright light emanating across so many furlongs. It spanned a thousand or more, at least.

He turned to look at the woman once more, to take in her face in hopes it spurred some memories. But he only saw worry. It drove her, guiding her to rash decisions like waking him early and rushing out the back exit of a cavern.

How do I know she speaks honestly? he wondered. How could he know if *any* of her words carried truth? He woke up, hatched, and she was there. She had brought him these strange clothes and this blade. He touched it reassuringly. At least he was armed in case something went wrong. He didn't even know her name, yet she talked about monsters attacking and a battle raging at the main entrance.

The man paused, listening to the night sounds. *If a battle were being fought nearby, I would hear its clanging of steel and blowing of horns.* Wars are always quite noisy, he knew that much, even if he could not remember his name, the name of his home near the mountains, or how he came to *hatch* from an egg.

"Prove it," he suddenly said, setting his feet firmly on the ground and drawing his knife from its sheath.

"Prove *what*?" the woman demanded, eyeing his blade cautiously.

"Prove there is a battle. Take me to it and show me on which side you fight. Perhaps you are tricking me, fighting against my allies."

"Allies?" the woman laughed. "You have no allies here except *me*."

"Then who fights the battle?"

She paused, looking around as if scanning the shadowy hills, but ignored his question. "This way," she finally said, pointing toward the glowing horizon.

"No." The man turned, walking the opposite direction.

"Come back!" the woman hissed, her voice commanding authority.

Her tone stirred another flash of images, of a small cabin in a tall forest, flanked by mountains on all sides. In it a girl and a boy argued, their voices carrying out into the night, dampened by steady rainfall that washed away everything but the siblings' anger.

Slowly, the man turned, his eyes full of shock as dozens of memories flooded in at once. He stared at his sister, entranced by her eyes now swirling like pools of blood, and lost himself in the horrors he suddenly remembered.

Behind her, a metal carriage topped the ridge, kicking up a cloud of dirt as it approached. It needed no horse to pull it, the thing was a metal beast of its own with two glowing eyes and four black wheels that sprayed rocks while skidding to a stop. Inside, a man leaned over and pushed open a door. He shouted something in a foreign language. It sounded odd, a blend of the rough Germanic spoken by Anglo-Saxons, but with hints and undertones of Latin.

"Speak Gaulish so he understands!" the woman commanded the newcomer.

"Get in!" the man said with only the slightest of accents. "They're coming!"

"You have to *help* me, Vince!" the woman pleaded. "He's remembering everything all at once!"

"Excellent timing," the man named Vince muttered, climbing from the vehicle and running to aid the woman. "Come on, kid," he urged. "It's gonna be a long night!"

Part I

Chapter One

Icy rain pelted a forested valley, coating it with misery. Beneath this cold sadness, villagers sheltered. Three days of wetness soaked thatch roofing, dripping steady droplets onto dirt floors. Yet the irritated people endured. They, who should be broken by the many hardships they suffered, accepted the onset of winter without complaint. Famine and plague had already visited and, more recently, war.

Rain was nothing new and neither was this misery, but the people of Cardac would never be free of the mud if their gods could not cease their endless weeping. That thought of gods further soured their moods. Inside their hovels, old and young alike huddled for warmth around hearths of stone, eyeing their dwindling supplies of firewood and lamenting that they would have to face the elements to collect more.

One such home had already sent a boy to gather.

Kado sat huddled under a tree, his back pressed hard against the bark and feet pulled close to keep his boots dry. In this moment he felt anger, not at the task nor against the gods, but toward his sister Briaca. He vented empty curses, each escaping his mouth as tiny puffs of fog.

"She's not my mother," he muttered. "I don't care that she's older and in charge." But she was and had been since the disappearance of Mother and departure of Father.

A thought struck him, igniting a spark that kindled fiery rage.

"I will be of age in two more summers," he realized. "Then I can leave her house and be accepted as a man in my own right." *And I will search for Mother and Father,* he vowed.

He turned dark eyes toward a pile of logs, chopped but not stacked, a meager collection considering the time he had already spent outside. He should find more, he knew, but the smoke billowing from his sister's chimney promised warmth and drew more than his gaze. Suddenly aware of how cold he truly felt, his muscles shivered and his teeth gave in to chattering.

The voice of Argant, the village teacher rang in his mind, a conversation from one of his many lessons. *A man always provides*, the old man had said, *thinking of family first and putting others before self.*

That had been when the lessons were still taught, before noblemen had conscripted the men and older boys as soldiers, taking them away from the village and into war. Cardac had not been the same since, left defenseless and without strength to toil. The task of replanting had fallen upon women, the old, and the very young for several springs. The work proved backbreaking and futile. Their most recent harvest, a meager one, was immediately claimed by the army.

Cardac would starve for at least another year.

Kado's hand wrapped tightly around his axe handle, worn and stained by years of Father's sweat and toil. *I'll find some more wood,* he thought, *enough I won't have to venture out again after rain turns to snow.* Careful not to ruin his boots or muddy the axe, he leaned against the tree and walked his feet into a better position to support his weight.

He stared down with sadness at the dark stain on the left boot. Footwear was valuable and these had once belonged to his father. Despite their worn and aged appearance, the leather held up and served him well against the rain and cold. But they were still a few sizes too large, and could easily slide off if sucked into a mud hole. That had already happened and was why he had rested to clean them under the tree. Father would be disappointed when he returned home... *if* he ever did.

Kado stepped from beneath the canopy, eyes misting and causing him to blink. Determined to finish the job, he scanned the forest floor for fallen branches. Finding one that would easily chop, the boy strode forward and raised the heavy tool above his head. Each time he brought it down he thought again about the boys he had once called friends, gone away and fighting alongside his father.

He suddenly realized his biggest problem was loneliness. As the oldest boy left in the village he was in between, older than the littles who still clung to their mother's aprons but still too young to be accepted as a man. He wished he still had a mother to cling to, but she had not loved her family enough. She had slipped away at night while her husband and children slept, leaving no warning or message, only her ghostly absence. Perhaps that was why Father left so willingly, leaving Briaca in charge.

His sister was loving but not kind. She resented her role, old enough to marry but with no men her age around to wed. Briaca wasn't ready to be a mother and often took out her mood on Kado, treating him even more like a child. But the world was not fair, neither to him nor her, and the situation was to blame, not his sister. Someday he would stand up for himself and tell her. He may not be a man, but Kado was sick of being a boy.

Even Argant cautioned against rushing responsibility. "Your time will come," the old storyteller always warned from behind his grey beard, leaning on his ivory staff as if he'd topple over any moment. "Don't be in such a hurry," he would say. "Focus instead on taking care of your sister by completing chores and helping around the house."

And so he did. Kado committed to the task at hand, gathering enough wood to last through the storm. Once he had loaded his spoils upon a sled, the boy followed the smoking trail leading upward from his sister's chimney. Each muddy step brought him closer to home.

Cries from the village caught his attention. It was difficult to make out their words, but someone spread alarm. Soon the ringing of bells joined the shouts, and Kado made a sudden dash for the house, careful not to let slip either his axe or the bundle of wood from his sled.

He arrived home just as Briaca stepped outside.

She wrapped a wool cloak around her shoulders. It was thin and moth eaten but was the warmest garment she owned. Her eyes betrayed worry.

"What's happening?" she asked Kado.

"I'm not sure." He let go the sled and grabbed Father's axe. With weapon aloft he offered, "Stay here and I'll go find out."

His sister's hand grabbed the long handle, wrenching the tool away and holding it firmly out of his reach. "No, you will go inside." Her eyes commanded obedience in that way she always did, reminding him he wasn't ready. "You'll get yourself killed just for holding this thing! What if it's Lars and you wave it at him? He'll gut you for sport!"

For a brief moment Kado stood with back straight, summoning enough courage to finally challenge his sister's authority. But then he sighed and visibly deflated. *She'll see me as a man someday, but not tonight,* he realized, and strode through the open door with slackened shoulders.

With a push Briaca let it slam behind him.

Once inside the boy felt the warmth of the hearth, suddenly feeling the dampness of his clothing. Shivering, he slipped from the soaked items and hung them near the fire. His father's boots were carefully placed far enough away they would not melt from the heat.

Dressed in a fresh tunic and britches, Kado pulled a chair as close as he dared to the flame. Picking up a kindling branch he poked angrily at the coals, sending embers racing upward like dazzling dragons dancing. These danced their courtship against a flaming sky while his mind wandered, dreaming of how splendid actual aerouants would be, a thrilling sight gliding and casting shadows over boring Cardac.

This had been his fantasy since childhood, a burning desire to find and bond one of the long, reptilian beasts. If he could, he would bend its mind to his will, forcing it to serve him like the legendary Erwan the Bold had done his at the height of Roman occupation, called the Age of Sorrows to the people of Gaul. That dream, to bond a dragon, was all he had left of Mother, the story she told her children each night before bed.

He wished that legends were more than stories. With a dragon under his command, he would return to Cardac and rain terror down upon Lars and his thugs. He would shout insults from atop the scaly back of the dragon, demanding the warlord bow in reverence before his beast. Maybe then his sister and the village would see Kado as a man instead of a boy, hailing his name as he flew away. Then he would seek out Lord Eduard and help him lead King Chilperic's army to victory, finishing the war so Father could return home.

The door abruptly opened, slamming against the wall. The boy jumped with fright. He spun around to face cold wind and rain forcing its way inside the hovel. Standing there as his sister strode in, he imagined himself a pitiful sight, a child wielding a pathetic stick like it were a sword. The tip, glowing red where he had poked the flames, broke off, landing on the tabletop and singeing it black. With a panicked hand he smacked out the embers before fire spread. The burning pain let him know how stupid he had been as he looked up, feeling small beneath Briaca's angry gaze.

"Pack a satchel," she commanded, pushing the door closed, her voice a mixture of fear and irritation.

"What happened?" Kado had never seen his sister so worried.

"No time to explain," she insisted, tossing bread and dried meats into a sack. "You have to leave *now*!"

"Where shall we go?" the boy questioned, suddenly less ready to be a man than he had earlier believed. That previous defiance had waned, replaced by fear. He put down the stick and grabbed Father's boots from the hearth, pulling them on.

"You're going alone," she insisted, "but only for a night or two. Lars is in the village, and he's looking for more boys for Lord Eduard's army. You're the oldest now, and they're coming this way."

"I can't go alone," he pleaded. "Come with me!"

Briaca's eyes betrayed her desire to do just that, to run for the hills and escape the warlord's reach, but she stubbornly held out a satchel of food and bloated waterskin.

"I can't leave you," Kado whispered, tears welling up and choking off whatever convincing he thought would change her mind.

"Run for the hills, find old man Argant, and hide out with him. I will find you after Lars has gone and it's safe to return," she promised.

Kado wrapped Briaca in a tight hug, gripping her fearfully while his heart raced to keep up with his thoughts. With no other option but obedience, he grabbed the satchel and fled into the storm. He felt neither rain nor chill as he ran southward, fueled by a burning desire to reach Argant and the safety the old man's cave would provide.

Chapter Two

Kado had only run a few miles before halting in his tracks. An icy film had coated the rocky hillside. He slipped, falling hard to the ground.

Only children flee trouble, he chided himself as he scrambled to his feet, turning to the north and staring in the direction of home. If he were a man instead of a child, he would have insisted she come with him. *No. If I were a man I would have joined Father in fighting the war!*

He stood there, torn between fleeing to the cave or facing Lars alongside his sister. In the end he decided he *would* hide out, but not without Briaca. He would go back for her. *I can't leave my sister. She's a woman!* He was man enough to understand what awful things Lars and his thugs might do to her body.

With determination, he began the northern trek toward home.

By now the rain had turned to sleet, pellets of ice pelting his face and souring his already foul mood. Pulling his hood lower to protect his eyes, the boy pushed onward, moving as fast as he dared without losing footing.

A scream sent him running, no longer worried for his own safety. Danger had found his sister. He followed the chimney smoke, lazily reaching over the treetops as if this were a normal evening. His eyes wanted to believe it had been nothing more than that, but the chilling sound of shouts and screams drew him to an awful scene.

"Get your hands off of me!" his sister demanded of her attackers. One of them let out a grunt, a sure sign she was fighting them off.

Maybe she doesn't need me, Kado wondered, but the truth made itself known the moment home came clearly into view.

He had been right to worry. Three men surrounded Briaca in front of an open door. Sounds of breaking pottery and overturned furniture revealed at least one thug was inside.

One of her attackers, a scrawny man with a crooked nose, lunged just as Briaca stepped aside, bringing her foot up hard to meet his groin. His knees buckled and the man collapsed, his spindly frame too encumbered with pain. A howling moan announced it would be some time before he could stand.

She gave him another kick for good measure.

Kado watched as one of the harassers swung a club, catching her off balance. With a thud it met the small of Briaca's back. She crumbled, breathless, unable to cry out.

The thugs quickly bound her hands and secured a hood over her head.

"No," Kado began to shout, but a frail hand grabbed his mouth and covered it tightly.

"Silence, fool!" the voice whispered loudly in his ear, the stench of its breath stale and unwelcome. "You'll bring them down quicker on us than you can save *her*!"

The boy lifted his eyes to meet those of Argant, the storyteller and lesson giver.

The hand slowly moved away and the boy started to protest, but a crooked finger shushed him to silence. "There are darker forces here than you know," the old man whispered.

"I know. Lars has come for fresh soldiers for the king."

"He wants more than soldiers," Argant spat. "I've been watching him and believe Lars is acting in his own interest." The old man's eyes darted toward the mountains far to the south. "Come, we have little time and must flee."

"Time already ran out, old-timer," a voice declared. Branches parted and a large man arrived. Long red hair clung to his shoulders as green eyes laughed at the boy. This man was tall, well-muscled and properly fed. He dressed as a nobleman, but Kado knew Lars wasn't truly noble stock. Merely standing beneath him caused the boy's knees to tremble. "You're a bit small to carry a pike, but you'll fetch a price for shining shields."

"Leave him be, Lars!" the storyteller spat. "You're here to fetch Lord Eduard and King Chilperic an army, not steal slaves for their camps!"

The warlord stood to his full height, a giant of a man in stature if not character. His laughing eyes were pools of darkness that matched his heart. "The rebellion needs all the help it can get, and everyone who can carry a blade is needed to finish pushing out the Romans!"

"Surely the war's not won!" Argant protested, genuinely shocked by the news. "The last I heard the Romans had Chilperic on his heels. The Emperor's face still graces our coins!"

Lars laughed out loud. "I take and spend *everyone's* coin, no matter the face on the metal. Besides, none of that matters. Chilperic is wounded and, with any luck, will die on the field. Lord Eduard leads and *will* win the war."

"Then you don't need this boy," Argant protested, "nor do you need the girl and those others taken from the village. I saw you loading them into wagons. Why do that if this war is won?"

The warlord narrowed his eyes, angrily weighing the life of this old man. "Lord Eduard owns this village and soon all of Gaul. His orders come down from higher even than Chilperic, and no old man will stop me from carrying them out."

"You can't have this boy," Argant insisted, his defiance showing Kado a glimpse of the younger man he once was. "You can't have that girl, either. Lord Eduard will need free people to tend his land when he *does* return home."

"You aren't listening! Chilperic was wounded in battle, is dying and almost dead," Lars sneered. "Eduard promised his land to me as a *fiefdom* once the king dies."

"Fiefdom? I don't know that word," Argant admitted.

"It's the first wave of progress after Eduard finishes Chilperic's battle and drives away the Roman's. These people are *my* property and I'll do with them what I please."

Kado could not believe his ears. If Lars claimed Cardac as his own, the villagers would suffer even worse after the war. "Tell your men to let my sister go," the boy demanded.

"Or what?" Lars sneered.

"Or I'll kill you myself," was the only threat Kado could muster. This made the big man laugh even harder, giving the boy a shove to the ground.

Kado's hands flailed as he toppled, reaching to grab ahold of the Argant's staff. As it fell away from his grip he found himself oddly staring at the ivory. Yellowed by age, strange carvings shone brightly white higher up the stave. The boy realized the entire staff must have once been splendid white. His head struck hard, his vision swimming to black as the world around him ceased to buzz. Even the sleet no longer bothered him. All feeling faded as consciousness fled.

Chapter Three

Kado awoke to humming, a strange, unexpected sound. Moments before he had stood face to face with Lars. Though he remembered the shove and his fall, he had no recollection of landing or anything thereafter.

Careful fingertips felt a sticky scalp, finding tenderness but no cuts.

The humming stopped. "Ah, good! You're finally alert!" Argant's voice echoed loudly between the boy's ears.

As his eyes opened, the boy realized more time had passed than first thought. He found himself lying in a cave next to a roaring fire. It flickered and danced upon a swirling breeze. Outside the entrance, the winds howled their anger, tossing large flakes of snow that had already piled taller than his father's boots.

"How luh... long," he stammered.

"How long what? How long have you been sleeping? Several hours. Or, do you mean how long it will take to fully heal your wounds? No one can prognosticate healing, for only the body itself knows."

Kado frowned. The old man was acting strangely aloof, as if he had not faced Lars and walked away. Oblivious to the weirdness of the situation, the old man sat bent over an open scroll that appeared nearly as ancient as his staff. That leaned against a rock nearby.

Briaca! Kado suddenly worried.

As if reading his thoughts, the old man said, "Your sister is fine, roughed up a bit and taken by Lars and his raiders, but unharmed. He carted off most of the women and children but is keeping her in the meeting lodge."

The boy sat up, the world around him swimming from the movement. "How do you know?" he demanded.

"I know a lot of things, Kado, son of Conrad." The man's face turned dark as he spoke, no longer aloof but full of hidden danger. "Or have you forgotten I taught the village lessons before war tore apart the land?" Gone was the frivolity in his demeanor, replaced instead by seething authority that demanded respect.

"No, I..." Kado had not meant to insult the old man who now appeared younger, full of strength and vigor, and no longer feeble and frail.

As soon as the change had come over Argant, it disappeared with a shrug and he added merrily, "Of course, I am *still* the storyteller as you villagers like to call me, despite my knowledge extends far beyond history and science. But as for *how* I know Briaca is safe, I will leave that detail out. Suffice knowing she has not been harmed." Argant finished speaking and returned his attention to the book, a sure sign he should not be further bothered.

Kado tried to stand but dizziness took over his legs.

"Rest, young one," the storyteller commanded. "You cannot seek vengeance with a fractured skull."

The boy's fingers reactively reached upward, probing the tender spot on his head.

"As to how I know your sister is unharmed, I said I will not speak. But to your current state of healing I will describe in detail. Lars left you for dead, not intending to do any harm greater than offer a fright. The icy ground added to your fall, and you struck your head on a convenient albeit ill-placed rock."

"Convenient?"

"Indeed," Argant agreed. "Had it not been there to knock a sizable crack in your noggin' Lars would have simply dragged you off with your sister. But heads have a tendency to bleed more than they should, and your accident lost any immediate usefulness you may have offered his cause. He left you for dead and in my charge."

Kado found the old man's words too much to bear. *Briaca is out there, taken but why?* He cringed considering the possibilities. *I have to save her,* he decided.

"So that's it?" the old man suddenly demanded, accusation looming in his tone. "You'll focus on saving your sister rather than avenging your entire village? What happened to your dreams?"

That the old man read his thoughts was no longer merely bothersome, it had grown downright terrifying. "Are you reading my mind?" Kado demanded.

The fire roared to life, angrily sending embers in every direction. The wind swirled the tiny crackles as if they had abruptly become living and taken flight.

Kado found himself entranced, watching the spectacle as he had earlier that day in his sister's home. Each tiny flame became a dancing aerouant, swirling around with long bodies pushed upward by slender wings.

"Do you see them?" the storyteller demanded.

"I see…" Kado was no longer sure what his eyes saw, only what his mind imagined. Hundreds of tiny dragons circled the cave, ducking and diving above the fire. Several came close enough to singe his cheeks, flushed by warmth and surging awe. "I don't know what I see," the boy lied.

Argant's voice grew louder, echoing throughout the chamber as he further accused, "You see what your heart desires, the tool of your vengeance. You yearn to be a bonded one, a vinculum to the aerouant!"

"I'm too young for vengeance!" the boy cried out.

"Too young?" the booming voice insisted. "Or too pathetic, too weak, and living in your sister's house? Living under *her* rule!"

"Stop!" the boy cried out, picking up a log and swinging it at the storyteller. The tip of it burned hot, a torch twisting flame into the visage of a dragon. The head of the shimmering beast looked up at the child, roaring scathing mockery. All at once Kado's thoughts from the morning rushed forward. He had called himself those same things and more. Now, looking down at the branch gripped tightly in his hand, the boy once more resembled a pitiful child wielding a pathetic stick.

"Why can't you become a man, young Kado?" the booming voice of Argant demanded. His face had twisted and grown in the shadows, reflected more like a demon than a man. "Why can't you be as Erwan the Bold?"

"I... I'm too young!" Kado protested, his temples pulsing with pain as Argant's voice rang with riotous laughter. He dizzied, the room swirling around him a cacophony of fiery dragons everywhere he looked. The intense gaze behind the cackling insanity, judged him each time Argant rushed by.

In the blink of an eye, the cave became as it was, a place of tranquility. The storyteller no longer loomed over the child. He sat reading his book. Even the dancing flames had subsided, softly crackling and no longer launching endless legions of dragons.

Only Kado had actually changed, standing where he had earlier lain, holding a flaming branch aloft and staring down at the shriveled, old man.

"Are you quite well?" Argant asked gently, looking up from his reading with a frown. "You don't mean to accost me with that torch, do you?"

Kado did not answer the question, choosing instead to ask one of his own. "If you are the storyteller, will you tell me one?"

"Of course, that is my purpose, is it not? Which story would you like me to tell?"

"I want to hear about Erwan the Bold."

As soon as he had spoken, Kado's torch snuffed into a swirling pattern of smoke.

Chapter Four

Argant quickly slammed the ancient book, so excited to tell a story he sent dust flying from its pages. Hopping to his feet he moved with renewed vigor, youthfully spry with a spring to every step. He whisked up the yellowed staff, swung it once in the air, and slammed its base hard against the rocky floor.

A deafening crack resounded, echoing like a thunderclap through the chamber and startling the boy. Kado felt his heart pound inside his chest as if it were a frog hopping free from danger. For a moment he forgot the tender spot on his skull, enraptured by the spectacle and feeling only excitement instead of pain.

"Erwan the Bold, you say?" the old man asked with a mummer's voice, leaning over the staff and grinning with hinted danger and thrilling adventure.

"Yes sir, if you would, please. It's been so long since I've heard it, I don't recall the details," the boy lied. He knew the story by heart, not only as a yearly tale at feast time, a remembrance of better times for the village, but from his mother's nightly tellings. To ask for it now surprised him, almost as much as the tiny visions still echoing in his eyes. If closed, he could still see the tiny aerouants flying around the cave.

"Erwan the Bold… Such a story, such a feat!" the old man muttered, gathering his wits as if trying to recall every detail about the adventurer. "A daring story for a boy carrying vengeance in his heart." He muttered to his staff as if in conversation. This built anticipation in the boy. Argant held up the staff, staring as if it were a puppet. "Where to begin?" he asked it. "We can begin with the original dragon sire and matron, the bestowers of wisdom to mankind!"

"Yes, please," Kado begged with earnest, he had never heard that story.

"No!" the old man screamed into the cave, his voice booming as it amplified through the chamber, growing with each echo. Turning slowly, he eyed the boy over his shoulder, holding the staff to his chest like Kado meant to grab it away. "You asked for Erwan the Bold, the embodiment of bravery, daring, and tenacity! The only man to fetter a dragon in a hundred years!"

"I'm sorry," Kado whispered, suddenly afraid he would hear no tale at all for his insolence.

Argant shrugged, his face kinder and again thoughtful. "No..." he mused. "You don't want a story of wisdom, you're too young and full of anger. What you need is something to feed that hatred for Lars, something to start you off on your own adventure," he accused, staring down at the boy with eyes full of madness. "A futile quest which will assuredly end in *death*."

Kado shivered at the word *death* and fear twisted his guts, tying them with knots impossible to unwind. The old man had spoken harsh truths. The boy *was* filled with anger, sought vengeance even, but cowardice would surely lock his feet in Cardac. He would never attempt to bond a dragon of his own.

Or would I? he wondered, feeling again that rushing thrill and imagining fiery aerouants flying all around. Their long bodies slithered through his mind with grand wings that pushed excitement to its limits. *No, I'm not a hero*, he finally decided. *I'm just a lost boy without parents, too afraid to stand up to my sister.* Thinking of Briaca sent surges of pain through his wounded head, a reminder he *did* have a mission of vengeance to undertake. He had no time for stories, he had to stand up to Lars and rescue her back. He stood and looked around for his satchel.

"Sit!" the old man commanded, and Kado collapsed immediately to the rocky floor.

The entire cavern transformed. The fire behind the boy roared, but the light around him softened as if hidden behind fogged glass. The walls reflected an eerie glow that seemed to ebb and flow with the storyteller's words. Only the staff in his hands retained its usual hue, an unshakeable yellow. Kado realized for the first time it may not be carved from ivory at all.

Argant held his staff like a scepter now, more than a walking stick, waving it over his audience as if the cave had been filled with hundreds of spectators instead of a single child. Basking in the conjured illusion of light, he seemed to grow in stature along with his voice. As he spread his arms wide they almost appeared to reach from wall to wall, his head seemingly brushing the stalactites above.

"Hear now the story of Erwan the Bold, chosen by dragons as rider of the aerouant! Our story ends with him called the Bold, but begins with a simple man with no titles. Listen now," the story-teller announced, "to the story of Erwan the Worthless, Erwan the Lamentable, Erwan of no consequence!"

Thus the story was told, with Kado hanging on every word. He almost felt like he had disappeared into the story itself.

"Erwan the Gaul had lived thirty years, an unremarkable servant of the Roman overseer, Dominus Titus. A man of no importance, blessed to a life of poverty as a lowly serf, Erwan wasted his youth tilling and sowing a land he could never own. Despite his station he lived his life with determined fashion, intent on experiencing each day to its fullest. He believed in his betters, trusted them, and remained fiercely loyal to the dominus—so much so that all he did was for Rome. Each row he plowed served the Empire, just as each word he spoke and every idea he conceived was in support of his lord and vassal. Despite his poverty Erwan enjoyed certain riches of the like the wretched Titus could only dream.

"This peasant, a man born without hope for personal wealth, eventually found pleasure in his poverty. He discovered joy and emotional wealth and happiness in the form of his lovely wife Adelia, a foreigner, from whence she came no one in the village knew. She eventually bore him two children, twins if the story be told correctly, a boy and a girl who filled their father's heart with joy.

"Each evening, upon the conclusion of his chores, young Rupert and sweet Racinda rushed down the path to greet and accompany their father to dinner. Only, on this fateful day, they failed to show up for their ritual, provoking Erwan the Boring to become Erwan the Lamentable. He found it odd, their lack of arrival, and quickened his pace to possibly reach them up the road or perhaps even at their hovel. They must have helped their mother too long with chores, or had been caught up in their playtime and lost track of time. With each step concern grew into worry, a condition parents often endure but shouldn't have to—usually the fault of the offspring, I'm sure. Eventually, Erwan's home came into view, and the sight he found horrified the father and husband, one which changed him forever. It *broke* him."

"Isn't this when he found their bodies?" Kado asked innocently, his excitement earning admonishment from the storyteller.

"I thought you didn't recall the details of this story," the old man accused.

"I, um, only assumed so because they hadn't shown up to greet him," Kado lied. He knew what happened. The Roman nobleman had seen the lovely Adelia in town and followed her home, demanding jus primae noctis despite he had not claimed it on hers and Erwan's wedding night. His men later murdered her and the children to hide the crime. It was a classic trope of storytelling, the catalyst by which the would-be hero is catapulted into his role.

Picking up where he left off, Argant told the story differently than Kado knew it.

"Heartbroken, Erwan came upon a frightful scene. Titus, it seemed, had a darkness lurking inside, a monster eager to satisfy his flesh by harming someone else's. Every unmentionable desire was satiated by his treatment of beautiful Adelia, and young Rupert and little Racinda also served to feed his hunger. He was a cruel man, one who left their bodies cold and lifeless without blood to warm them in the afterlife."

Kado, mortified by the obvious change in the story, sat aghast, his face filled with disbelief. "No!" he screamed. "How *dare* you change the story! He came home to find Titus had taken her for pleasure. The Roman soldiers killed Adelia and the children to hide their lord's crime!"

The storyteller's mood darkened, his voice booming with sadness and lamentation. "You *have* heard this tale before, but what you know is an improper telling! You demanded the *truth* and so you shall have it entirely!"

Kado recoiled, seeing Argant with newfound sight. There *was* a truth to his words, he could sense it. "How do you know these details?" the boy demanded.

"Wisdom, child. I hold wisdom unlike any man can fathom!" It took several seconds for the echo of his statement to subside, the flames once more settling soft shadows upon the storyteller's countenance.

He resumed telling the story, describing how Erwan arrived just as Titus had finished his meal, stepping onto his carriage as the peasant approached his hovel.

"'Deal with him,'" Titus commanded his soldiers. 'I no longer desire a taste for blood,'" the storyteller said with dark evil in his voice.

"After Dominus Titus had fled, Erwan fought and killed the guards, then rushed into his home to find his family had been drained of their lifeforce, empty husks sapped grey by a monster."

"Titus was a voltur?" Kado exclaimed, using the term for the undead and their insatiable lust for fresh blood.

"Similar, but not quite. Dominus Titus had an ailment, his body lacking nutrients only gained from drinking human sanguis, but, at the time, he was most certainly as mortal as Erwan the Bold eventually proved."

"Why didn't he kill Titus on the spot, as soon as he found his family?" the boy asked with disbelief. If it had been *his* family, he would have turned stark raving mad in an instant.

"The Roman soldiers were accustomed to the reactions by peasants to their lord's dalliances. They beat poor Erwan with their gauntlets, leaving him to lie on the ground, presumably killed. But they underestimated his resilience and determination to live."

All at once the flames stoked and the cavern glowed with firelight. Argant, no longer a giant among men, again appeared a tired old man. He leaned against his staff, his legs no longer bearing his weight.

Kado stared at the instrument, now certain it was not made of ivory but something quite similar. The yellowish hue had grown darker since the story, the carved runes along its spine now shining starkly white in contrast.

"What did he do next?" the boy asked in a whisper, convinced the rest of the story would differ from the earlier versions as well.

"Erwan the Despondent, now fully pathetic, climbed to the highest peaks of Mount Sapientia."

"To find and bond the aerouant?" Kado assumed.

"No, boy! To cast his pitiful existence off a cliff!" With the wave of his staff the fire snuffed nearly to extinguished. "Now, the hour is late and your wound has healed, so it's time to sleep. You will need whatever strength rest has to offer."

Kado reached cautious fingers to probe his injured skull, shocked to discover it no longer throbbed. Gone too was the supple tenderness, replaced instead by freshly firmed scalp. "How?" he marveled, but the old man gave no answer. He had rolled over and faced the far wall, his mysterious staff gripped tightly against his chest.

The remaining story of Erwan the Bold would have to wait until morning.

Chapter Five

Kado awoke to a howling of wind, his body shuddering against unbearable cold. Rolling over he stoked the fire, lazily adding another log and a bit more kindling to push it along. The wind currents added extra fuel. Where once the air had softly breezed, it now churned and disturbed everything in its path. As the tiny flames leapt upward he noticed an empty spot where the old man had slept.

Argant was gone.

Blinking his eyes into focus the boy scanned the cavern, quickly discovering the reason for the swirling breeze. The rock wall against which the old man had slept had opened into a narrow passage. Dust and snow flurries mixed in the current as tiny orbs danced deeper into the waiting abyss.

Kado scrambled to his feet, examining the spot where Argant had slept. No trace of the man remained.

Next he investigated the opening. What had earlier been solid rock proved merely a façade, easily moved aside with pressure in a precise spot. With a heave the boy opened it wider, inviting more winter wind into the cavern. The fire abruptly blew out.

He quickly fashioned a torch, wrapping cloth around a tree branch. Looking around he found the discarded portions of a meal—several pieces of bone with fatty meat still clinging. Rubbing the greasy tallow hard into the fabric he fueled the wick, touching his torch to the dying embers while blowing softly. It finally ignited.

The boy scurried after the old man.

The wide passage led downward, deep into the hillside. Kado grew more anxious with each step, the cool breeze licking at the torchlight as much as it chilled his skin.

What if the storyteller is angry I followed, he wondered, suddenly fearful of the old man's magic. *He's more than he seems.*

The moisture in the air grew thicker the deeper he stepped, musty and strangely foul. It felt more like a tomb than a cavern. Each step brought trepidation, promising danger loomed ahead.

Danger, the boy wondered, *or adventure?*

Argant had been correct; Kado lusted for vengeance and Lars must die. *I'm too young to fight him now, on my own,* he knew. But that would change if he traveled to Mount Sapientia. Dragons waited there, the wise creatures of legend who would bond with a human if their purpose proved worthy. Dragons were supposed to be powerful, indestructible even, through strength as much as with their magic.

The old man's staff is proof that magic exists. It isn't made of wood, nor is it ivory... what is it? he wondered.

Kado's eyes had grown more accustomed to the flickering torchlight, now seeing each footfall more clearly. He moved more quickly. Emboldened by confidence and fueled by excitement, he nearly ran as he rushed downward, no longer afraid of what waited up ahead.

Argant knows the rest of the story, the real *story, of how Erwan the Bold earned the trust of an aerouant.* He had to find him, to demand the rest of the tale and...

The boy gasped. The tunnel had opened suddenly into another cavern, vast and more magnificent than the one above. The cool darkness wrapped him in silence.

He proceeded carefully, holding the torch with an outstretched arm. It only lit a small portion of the cavern, hiding whatever waited, and he could only view a dozen or so strides at a time. Who knew what dangers lurked—there could be pitfalls, creatures, or poisons meaning to do him harm. Panic set in, that overwhelming desire to be anywhere other than this cave. His heart threatened to leave its place in his chest, pounding so hard it might flee toward freedom.

I must return above, he urged himself, but his feet carried him forward. Soon he had no sense of direction, unsure which way even led him back. The trail was lost in the void all around.

No! Kado scolded his cowardice. *Briaca needs me, so does Father! So even might Mother, wherever she may be.* It was up to him now, the boy who wanted so badly to become a man. *They all need my vengeance, the entire village does! Only I am in a position to free them from Lars!*

These thoughts pushed him forward, the desire to bring righteous anger to the warlord. Once bonded with a dragon he would have that power and more, to preside as judge over the man's evil and pass judgement against his life.

Lars will beg me, 'Kado please don't kill me, please don't have your dragon eat me!' But I will remember how he stole away Briaca and tried to take me away, too. I will avenge Father fighting for the king, and also Mother... oh, where are you mother?

"Yes!" Argant's voice bellowed through the cavern. "That is the vengeance you must have! Fuel it! Make Lars pay!"

The darkness disappeared, replaced by light so brilliant he could barely look at the fires springing up all around. Kado squeezed his torch, rendered so useless by the brightness. He tried to open his eyes against the pain, but they refused.

"Bond your dragon and convince it to rip Lars in two halves!" the storyteller urged.

Kado finally managed to blink the cavern into focus. It was larger than he ever believed could exist underground, with towering walls reaching ever upward. The vastness overwhelmed him, but what lay in the center caused whimpering fear to catch in his throat. The boy urged his body to turn and run away, but his feet had planted firmly.

Argant stood over the colossal remains of a dragon, his arm outstretched and holding his staff. Its yellowish tinge matched the skeleton exactly. That's when Kado understood its origin. *It isn't wood nor ivory, it's* dragon *bone!*

The story of Erwan the Bold instantly turned from myth to truth in is mind. The many fires flickered then surged brightly several times, casting strobing shadows around the chamber. Within their flashing the skeleton seemed to move, stretching out its neck toward the boy.

It roared, blowing back his hair while sharp teeth snapped at his head. Its attack forced him to cower. Hiding behind his pathetic torch he once more felt like a useless child standing before a mighty aerouant.

"Vengeance!" it roared angrily, its ancient breath snuffing out all the light in the room.

The branch no longer burned but smoked, swirling foulness that blew back at the boy. He scanned the darkness, trying to remember where Argant had stood. A soft glow slowly appeared from that direction, the tip of his staff now a beacon replacing darkness. With shadows dancing on his face the old man stood beside the skeletal beast, his own eyes resembling torches of their own.

"But first you must go," the old man urged, "and climb Mount Sapientia just as Erwan did so many years ago."

"How?" Kado asked. "What did he do once he reached the top? How is a dragon even bonded? What do I do once I've found one?"

Argant smiled at the boy, hiding a secret behind laughing eyes of fire. "Only a dragon rider knows how, or *everyone* would do it!"

"I've seen the mountain with Father, once when he took me to Aventicum for King Chilperic's coronation. We left Cardac *after* the spring planting, and there was still snow on the top! I never saw a dragon fly over it, though. Are they always there?"

The old man found humor in the child's chatters and broke out in rippling laughter. His voice echoed through the cavern. With the wave of his staff the skeletal dragon stood, shook off dust from its bones, then fanned out skinless wings. These beat against the air with force, pushing it upward until disappearing in the shadows above.

Kado squinted and focused on a bit of yellow left behind on the floor. "What is that?" he asked.

"Step forward and take it," Argant commanded.

Heavy with apprehension he crept slowly, moving forward until the object became clear. It was a single tooth, perfectly hollow and rounded to a point. Its color matched the old man's staff. A trembling hand reached to pick up the tooth, feeling its smoothness everywhere except the sharp tip. There he cautiously felt the ragged edges of a small cavity on the side.

"What do I do with it?"

"The same thing Erwan did, boy! Call forth the dragons to be judged!"

"But I've no idea *how* to judge a dragon, much less to call one."

Argant laughed again, the light of his staff abruptly snuffing the room to darkness. As the echo of his voice faded, Kado realized he had slipped away, leaving the boy alone to ponder the meaning of it all.

"I *will* avenge you, Briaca!" he shouted into the darkness.

From high up, hidden in the shadows, a dragon answered with a roar.

Chapter Six

The room plunged into darkness. Terrified, Kado dropped the useless remains of his torch and clung to the dragon's tooth. Just as suddenly as the roar subsided, shrieks echoed through the chamber. Clicking and clacking turned into a sound the boy found oddly familiar, like teeth chattering in winter. At first he thought it might be his own, but soon a horrible scream erupted, a noise so shrill every hair stood on his neck. He turned, searching for steps to retrace but found no sign of the entrance.

Another trilling cry came from high above, sending Kado rushing toward a hopeful exit. With one hand outstretched he ran, crashing hard against stone. Pain screamed through his palm and wetness trailed down his arm. Instead of an opening he had found only rocky wall. Panic set in, sending his fingers into a furious shuffling while still clutching the dragon's tooth.

Which way? he wondered, frantically feeling both directions but finding no hole in the wall. Right or left both felt the same.

Another roar, much like the first, coursed terror through his body. Kado hurriedly sped his search. The angry bellow subsided and, at the end of the exhalation, a distinct sucking of air readied the monster for another cry. The boy whimpered with anticipation, squeezing hard against the wall. Filled with terror, tears welled upon his cheeks. When it finally came, the roar filled the entire cavern with brightness, a torrent of dragon flame lighting both ceiling and walls. The heat of it warmed the boy's skin and chilled his spine.

In that brief light he found the passageway. Now free of the cavern and its horrific nightmare, Kado's feet carried him swiftly through the darkness, racing upward to waiting freedom. Where once he felt dread, relief rushed in.

The way up took longer than the way down, despite he ran full speed. Soon his lungs hurt from the effort. With a racing heart Kado collapsed to his knees. His head turned every direction, both eyes searching but again finding only darkness. There should be an opening up ahead, the way he had entered, and surely it must be lit by the arrival of dawn.

His thoughts turned to home.

Fear is all in your mind, but dangerous all the same, his father's voice echoed inside his head. *Pain is real but fleeting, it harms us less than fear.*

Drawing a deep breath helped slow his pulse, pushing that feeling aside.

Very good, son, his father's voice whispered kindly.

"I miss you so much," Kado said aloud. "I wish you weren't away fighting the war."

The inky blackness changed, shimmering and growing noticeably warmer. The boy wavered, the heat now searing his skin like the dragon fire had in the cavern below. Only, now it felt different. He paused, standing perfectly still while peering into the blackness. One by one, ghostly fires appeared all around him, illuminating row after row of army tents. His father sat before one, quietly sipping tea from a tin mug.

"My son and daughter are all alone," Conrad told his companion, a man dressed in the same pikeman's cote. "That's who I'll return to after the war."

"No missus?" the other soldier asked.

"She went away." His father replied in the same manner he had always answered Kado and Briaca, without emotion and not wishing to elaborate.

"What does that even mean?" the soldier laughed, earning hushing sounds from the other fires. Quieter he asked, "Why would your wife just leave?"

"She had… She had something. Some pressing obligation to take care of, a task more important than anything else she could do as a wife or mother."

"And you let her go?"

"I couldn't stop her. She left in the night without leaving a note."

Before the other pikeman could respond, horns echoed in the distance. As both men looked upward their eyes grew wide, reflecting tiny fires descending from the sky above.

"Take cover!" someone in the camp shouted, and the whistling of arrows sounded overhead.

Conrad rolled next to the tent, pressing his body close, but his friend was not so lucky and found no such cover. A flaming arrow entered his chest with an audible *thwack*. Without another word he collapsed beside the cookfire.

"No!" Kado screamed, his voice echoing through the tunnel as the vision faded into blackness.

"Get moving!" a voice roared, booming through the passage. It had possibly been that of Argant, but the pounding in the boy's ears made it difficult to tell. Up ahead, a sliver of light revealed the opening.

The boy sprinted as fast as he could, skidding to a halt when the tunnel again changed, morphing into the forest around Cardac. The sun had nearly risen in the eastern sky, casting warmth on the light snowpack coating rooftops and the ground between homes.

Creeping forward he pushed a ghostly branch away from his mouth, feeling others scrape the skin along his arms. Looking down, his eyes grew wide with surprise to find blood oozing slightly from the tiny cuts. This vision, whatever it truly was, seemed as magically real as the blood trickling down his arm. He was about to step out onto the roadway into town when voices locked his feet firmly into place.

"That's all we can manage from here?" Lars asked, stepping out from the temple. One of his thugs followed closely behind.

"We found Cardac *lacking* to say the least," the henchman explained. His slender build and crooked nose starkly contrasted the athletic and ruggedly handsome warlord he addressed.

Kado waited till both men passed his patch of thicket before following. They continued their conversation the entire way to the meeting house. Hanging back and keeping behind cover, Kado listened closely.

"We sent the women to Aventicum and the children to work your manor. But there is one slave worth keeping, and that's the girl we found outside of town."

The girl? Kado wondered if they meant Briaca.

"Why would we keep *her*?" Lars demanded.

"At first we thought she might fetch a good price from a nobleman as either a governess or a house servant. But she proved wild, slashing and gnashing with her teeth—even clawed like a wildcat once unbound."

"All the more reason to send her off," Lars insisted. "Other than needing a good breaking in, she would have sold well. Why didn't you ship her off with the others?"

"We *had* planned to cart her to Aventicum, but there's something… unusual about her. I can't put my finger on it and think you should examine her yourself."

"I've got too much of my own to deal with," Lars snapped, "and have no time to bother with a slave!"

A branch broke beneath Kado's feet. He paused, holding his breath and praying to the gods the men did not notice.

But somehow Lars had heard. Without warning, the man whirled around and looked directly where the boy stood. He stepped forward, coming closer but looking straight through him.

At first Kado thought he was seen, but stood too frozen by fear to turn and flee.

"I know you're here, whoever you are," the warlord whispered. "I just don't know how." Lars sniffed deeply then blinked, cocking his head as if listening. His breath had turned shallow as if excitement or fear had come upon him. Suddenly his face contorted, the bones twisting and churning as if growing thicker and longer. Two of his teeth became like fangs, drooping low across his lower lip. "And I smell *dragon* on you!" the warlord added.

As quickly as Lars had changed he was the same. He shrugged and turned, continuing with crooked nose toward the meeting house. He lifted his head only once, to view the rising sun breaking over storm clouds. After a pause he casually swept off an inch or two of snow from the top of a barrel, tossing it into the air as he said, "I think I *will* examine her, after all. Besides, we'll be wintering here in Cardac, and I may find her *entertaining*."

The vision completely faded, just like the first, and morning sunlight disappeared completely into the darkness. Kado once again set off running, the tunnel no longer seeming as long as it previously had.

Out of breath he reached the cavern above, basking in the light of dawn but chilled by a breeze made frigid after passing over a fresh blanket of snow. So much of it had fallen overnight and the valley between the cave and Cardac glowed with eye-squinting brilliance.

At the entrance he found a gift left by the old man, a satchel of food still tied by Briaca's hand. Next to that lay a full waterskin and a small, steel dagger resting atop a fur cloak. From this vantage point the boy looked north toward his sister, praying he would find her in time. Off to the east he viewed the same storm Lars had seen from Cardac and shivered. Kado was running out of time and would need to travel south if he hoped to climb Mount Sapientia before the worst of the storm arrived.

Without even a glance over his shoulder he stepped out from the cave, taking with him the items Argant had laid out for him to carry. Not knowing what purpose it might serve, he tucked the dragon's tooth neatly into the sack then retied the opening.

His first real adventure had begun.

Chapter Seven

Kado reached Mount Sapientia by late afternoon, the forest thinning as he reached the base. What he found proved impossible to climb. The sheerness of the rocky outcropping stretched forever upward, a cliff he could not attempt to scale. Nature had already coated the highest peak with a blanket of snow and ice. The slickness of every hand or foothold appeared treacherous and, even if he managed to get to the higher rocks, a storm had topped the summit that would worsen conditions and threaten certain death.

Dismay filled the boy, a half day's walk in the wrong direction of town wasted on dreams of dragons. Pulling his cloak tightly around his shoulders, he stared upward, hoping to find an easier path. This delay might have saved him his life. After several minutes of shivering, the young man decided to weather out the coming storm by finding shelter. He chose a spot nestled between two rocks, hoping they would block the worst of the winds. Overhead, a tall fir kept him dry.

Thankfully, the fallen wood he found here was seasoned, igniting easily upon a bed of dry kindling. By evening he had a sizable fire by which to keep warm. Less than an hour later the storm had fully arrived, shaking the tree above as fierce winds howled down the mountain face.

He spent this time trying to remember the rest of the tale of Erwan the Bold. After the changes the storyteller had made, especially the dark revelation about Dominus Titus being like the voltur, he began to question every part of the legend he knew. Most importantly being *how* the hero had climbed Mount Sapientia.

In the story he heard as a boy, including the version retold over and over by his mother, Kado could have sworn Erwan had found a path. There was no scaling involved, no climbing, and no threat of falling. But now, facing the sheer rock face, he saw no other option. To do so, especially with the rocks coated in ice, would mean certain death for anyone who tried. Staring deeply into the fire and huddling close to its warmth, he tried to remember the exact wording as it was told.

The first part came easiest. After Erwan had found the bodies of his wife and children, *sucked dry by Dominus Titus,* Kado marveled, casting aside his belief they had simply been murdered by a tyrant, the farmer had packed supplies and hiked south to the mountain. The only weapon he carried had been a simple scythe. Patting his satchel, the boy had a steel knife and a dragon's tooth. He would have rather had a scythe.

Kado found the rest of the details lacking. Worse, murkiness shrouded the story itself. Supposedly, Erwan had reached the mountain by nightfall and decided to rest and attempt the climb at first light.

At least I share in that problem, the boy mused.

He closed his eyes, listening to the creaking trees and wailing winds. He too would have to venture out the next day. The problem, Kado discovered, was the timing. Erwan had set out on his journey in spring, right after planting, while this boy journeyed at the onset of winter. The path may have been easier to find without the snow.

After several minutes of pondering, the winds lulled Kado into slumber. Along with sleep came dreams...

Kado, a woman's voice echoed in his mind. *Why don't you remember the words of the story as I taught you?*

Mother? the boy asked the phantom. *Why did you* leave? *You've been gone two years!*

Ignoring his question, she asked again, *Do you forget my words?*

Hearing her voice helped and brought him back to a place from his childhood. Sitting upon his mother's lap he could smell the earthy tones of her hair, skin, and clothing. The familiarity of it brought forth a surge of emotion, choking him briefly with tears and forcing him to swallow and breathe.

He looked down, finding a younger version of Briaca sitting cross-legged in front of the hearth. Her eyes were large with interest, listening intently to the story their mother told. She briefly broke them away to meet his, giving her little brother a wink and smile.

These were the best years when their entire family was still together. All Kado needed now was to see Father. That wait was not long and soon the door opened. A large man appeared, his dark beard wild and full and giving him a bearish appearance. Only his eyes were gentle, a soft hazel as kind as Briaca's.

Everyone looked up when he arrived, and Mother briefly paused her tale.

"Don't let *me* interrupt the story of Erwan the Bold!" he roared, giving his wife a kiss on the cheek before patting the head of each child. Briaca wrapped her arms around his leg and hugged it tightly. Kado focused on his father's boots, newly made and not yet weathered by time.

Mother continued, "He emerged from the forest, facing a rocky wall that seemed to reach the heavens. Erwan stared up at the peak high above, desperate to scale the wall in a single bound. But night impeded his travels, him having spent all day burying his wife and children."

"And so he rested," Father added from across the room, "as all good fathers should after a long day." He gestured to his boots, raising one into the air, and Kado hopped from Mother's lap, racing to do his nightly task. Turning away from father he straddled the boot, gripping the heel of it with his hands. Father gently placed the other boot against his son's buttocks and pushed, sending the boy toppling to the floor amid gleeful laughter. Briaca rushed to remove the other in the same way. "Go on, dear," Conrad urged his wife with a broad grin, "please continue."

"And so he rested," she agreed. "He camped all night on the edge of the forest and awoke at first light. Heartbroken, he found the mountain had not changed. There was no scaling the slippery rocks, and no other way up and around the barrier."

"But he found a way!" little Kado exclaimed, climbing once more onto his mother's lap.

"Yes, there is always a way around a problem if you know where and when to look," she agreed. "As the sun rose higher he stared upward, building the courage to climb. Just as he was about to attempt what would surely result in death, he found the path. Upward he walked all morning and afternoon, very careful not to look down. He did only once, and the vertigo of that single misstep shook him, nearly costing his life, but he eventually reached the summit."

"And then he found dragons!" Father roared, standing and raising his arms like a monster. Kado and Briaca laughed and scrambled to get away as he chased them both to bed. Catching each one with a giant hug, he devoured them kisses before tucking them in.

"Finish the story, Mother!" Kado begged his mother from the safety of his blankets.

"Tomorrow I will. Everything is better when fully revealed by first light," she said with a smile.

Kado, suddenly realizing things were not as they seemed, remembered he wasn't a little child, and both Mother and Father were actually gone away. As if the phantoms could read his thoughts, both physically changed in his dream vision. His parents physically twisted and contorted before his eyes, just as Lars had in his vision, and were no longer themselves but gaunt creatures with spindly arms and legs. Their ribs sunk as if malnourished, their bloated bellies bulging from want.

One of the demons, that which once was his father, sneered with tight lips stretched across bloodstained teeth. Sharp canines slowly grew before Kado's eyes, stretching downward from the gums above, scraping the bottom lip and drawing a line of blood. The voltur licked the injured spot, tasting its own blood and salivating for more.

"He's awake," the creature informed the other, its voice booming in the boy's ears.

Kado's eyes opened, finding the hellish nightmare had followed him into the world of the living. Both voltur had joined him in the tiny shelter. One stood over him while the other ransacked his belongings.

"Food, food, food, and more food," the second creature complained, tossing the dried meats, fruits, and nuts aside. "Why can't humans carry anything of value like a *fresh* kill? It's bad enough they don't eat it raw, but to dry it out?"

"Stay out of my things!" Kado screamed trying to scramble to his feet. The first voltur pushed him hard against the rocks, surprisingly with the strength of five men. The resulting impact took the boy's breath away, leaving him gasping and holding the back of his head.

The creature moved faster than anything the boy had ever seen. In one moment it stood over him, and in the next it was atop his chest, gnashing fangs biting at his neck.

Kado struggled to hold it off, feeling its hot breath moving closer as he grew weaker. A bit of warm drool landed on his neck, warning the bite was next.

"Stop!" the second creature suddenly cried out, pulling something from the satchel.

The ravenous creature turned, angrily baring its fangs at the interruption, and froze. Kado could not see its expression, but felt its grip tighten. All of a sudden it let go entirely. "A dragon's tooth!" it exclaimed. Without diverting its eyes from the object, it demanded from Kado, "Where did you find one of those, boy?"

"I'm a friend of the aerouants!" Kado lied, hoping to scare the voltur away. To his surprise this only seemed to increase their interest. They alternated looking at him, the tooth, and then at each other. Each time he caught their glance he realized his chances of being eaten diminished. *They must be afraid,* he thought.

Finally, the voltur on his chest spoke. "Let's go," it insisted, "quickly!"

"But we haven't fed!" the other complained. After a few moments of silence, it cocked its head then bared its fangs. With a nod it abruptly hurried from the shelter. A heartbeat later the voltur atop Kato had disappeared as well. The boy gasped at the sudden intake of air, free of the weight that had squeezed most of it out.

They're afraid of dragons! he reveled, laughing aloud as soon as he was able.

But the hour was either late or early depending on one's perspective, and the boy did not go back to sleep. He sat with his back to the rocks, holding his small dagger forward in case the creatures returned. He stayed this way until daybreak.

Chapter Eight

Dawn did not arrive fast enough for Kado. Fear kept him awake several hours more, stoking his fire and thinking about his mother's words. He finally relaxed at first light, confident the voltur had moved on. These creatures of the night despised the sun.

It burns them, his mother taught him long ago.

Until now he had believed voltur were nothing but boogeyman stories told to keep children inside at night. But now he had seen their sickening gauntness firsthand, touched their shrunken skin, and smelt the awfulness on their breath. It was of death and decay, their very existence mocking the living.

But they fled after finding the dragon's tooth, he remembered.

That thought had warmed him through the remainder of night, with his cold hand clutching the relic in his lap while the other gripped the little dagger which he hoped would fend off the creatures till morning. He knew every inch of the tooth by now, from the wide hollow opening to the little chipped cavity near the tip. Several times he had imagined what the teeth of his own dragon would look like, how sharp they would be, and if that sharpness would be enough to devour any voltur who dared bother a vinculum.

I'm certain of it, he decided, *for the creatures to have left so quickly.* He surmised dragons must be the ancient enemy of the voltur. *Surely dragons are the stronger of the two.*

Kado waited till the sun had fully peeked over the horizon before venturing out. Eager to view the rocks in the morning light, he, like Erwan the Bold, prayed the path would be easier to see.

It was not.

All that hope and excitement, all that which kept fear at bay, collapsed in a single moment. The storm had encased the entire rock face in ice, making it fully impassable. It was no easier to climb than the evening before and had grown so much worse. All he could do was stare, hoping to glimpse a change, any at all, as the sun rose into the morning sky.

The story was a lie, he concluded. *There's no way Erwan found a path!*

But what should he do? Perhaps he stood in a different spot than Erwan had so long before. Maybe the mountain itself had changed. Rocks do fall, after all. Perhaps he could circle the mountain and seek a pass elsewhere.

No, this is where he found the path! It must *be!*

He had all but given up when his stomach growled. He grabbed his satchel, diverting his eyes from the cliffside to look inside for some breakfast. His mouth watered at once over the dried meat, the first bit of food he found appealing in two days. Biting a bit of it off the larger piece, he gave the mountain one more appraising look.

The sun had risen higher in that moment he looked for food and now cast shadows along the rocky face. A darker area zigzagged all the way to the top, unbroken.

Kado froze, his mother's words echoing in his mind. *Everything is better when fully revealed by first light,* she had said. It appeared she spoke wisdom.

Surely it's not this easy, he thought, but from this vantage point it seemed as if the sun had shown him the way up. Scooping up his satchel, he ran to the base and its slippery starting point.

Was it really the way up?

It could *be,* he realized, if he could only get about ten feet higher. From there he thought he could see a flat ridge leading upward at a reasonable grade. *If I can only climb to that spot!* Pulling out his dagger he turned it over, hitting it against the rocks to break apart the ice. Once he had uncovered a few hand and footholds, he sheathed it and began the climb.

He proceeded easier than expected, and soon he stood on what really was a ledge. It wasn't wide, only enough so he could stand with both feet together, but maintained the same breadth all the way up for several strides. There, it seemed to disappear but, knowing now what to look for, he found another ledge a little further up.

There really is *a path!* he rejoiced, following in the footsteps of Erwan the Bold.

He reached halfway to the top when he fully lost sight of the ledge. Panic set in quickly, the fast pumping of his heart taking over the thoughts between his ears. It was hard to breathe, both from the cold and the dizzying height. He made the mistake of looking down, thinking maybe he should retrace his steps to find a way he had missed. From this height all that did was make him sway, blackness dancing at the edge of his vision.

He felt himself falling, the weight of his small satchel pulling him downward. If he lost his footing he would die, so Kado reached both hands toward the icy wall. One of them found a dry spot to hold on to and, with a gasp, he hugged the rocks. Panting, thankful to not have fallen, he questioned his sanity for attempting this climb.

What am I doing? he asked himself. *A strong wind could send me over the side!* He was going to fall—that had become his reality.

After several slow breaths he willed himself to try again and look around. In that moment the sun peaked out from a cloud, shining its warmth on another rocky ledge only a few feet up from the one on which he stood. He could reach it, if he pushed forward just a bit... but he would also need to step across.

One foot. Two. He moved.

As he came closer he realized the ledges had once been connected. Somehow, a portion had broken away between both sections, leaving behind this small gap.

If Kado were full grown he might have had an easier time, but his feet had to stretch, finding another handhold halfway above while hugging the cliffside. This time he kept his eyes locked upward, afraid to let them drift groundward.

The handhold turned out another ledge, a depression in the rocks into which he pulled his body. The rocks had been carved, it seemed, by sharp tools. *Or dragon talons!* the boy imagined. This would have been the perfect spot to stay and rest had he not been so intent on reaching the summit. He gave it a thorough once over, looking for any artifact which may have belonged to Erwan, but came away with nothing but dust and debris.

Afraid to waste any more time, he pressed on, stooping low to the edge of the small cavern, standing nearby the higher ledge. He would have to jump from here and chose a landing spot with great care. As he made the final hop he let out a joyous battle cry, his voice echoing into the valley below. He landed with surer footing than he expected and grinned at his audacity. Safe on the other side, he breathed long and slow breaths of victory.

But how will I get down? he wondered. But then he knew. *I will have a dragon, and I will* ride *him to Cardac!* He wouldn't have to climb back down at all, nor would he have to repeat these acrobatics, not once he accomplished his task. Success was as simple as bonding his dragon.

The rest of the climb brought him closer to the summit, closer to his goal, and with each step his heart grew more excited.

I'm so close, I should hear them soon!

The thought of a dragon's roar filled him with wonder. What will their scales feel like? Will they be as afraid of him at first as he is of them? What if they *ate* him? That final thought was one he hadn't considered in this entire quest. He briefly panicked; it could all go wrong. They may not bond with him at all.

But Erwan had succeeded. His aerouant chose him as vinculum and he *made it down!*

Reaching the final stretch, that last few steps, Kado moved faster, desperate to get off this ledge. He nearly ran.

Chapter Nine

The summit of Mount Sapientia opened into a circular valley, the likes of which Kado had never imagined. Despite sitting so high above the tree line, a forest thrived. The boy marveled at the strange trees, so different than the needle bearing pines below. These were tall and broad-leafed, their canopy shading a bed of flora surrounding broad trunks. Most amazing was how the snow had fallen during the storm, completely encircling the valley but refusing to touch this forest. The white blanket clung only to the tallest, outermost edges, falling as warm rain upon the wide center.

Kado slowly stepped downward into the valley, aware of a strange warmth emanating from the ground beneath his feet. Overhead, colorful birds called out to one another, warning of snakes slithering up branches for a meal. Even the insects were odd atop Mount Sapientia, with colorful beetles waddling between the ferns and brightly painted butterflies flittering in the air.

The boy pushed toward the lowest part of the valley, certain he would find the dragons resting there. *They will be grand,* he imagined, *like when Erwan found them.* The monstrous beasts would be impossible to hide. He expected lumbering giants as tall as the trees but, as he stepped into a wide clearing, he found only rocks.

Nothing grew here and the ground was smooth obsidian. Even these volcanic mounds were unusual, tall forms wider across then he could reach, leftover from some ancient eruption. Most frustrating was the stark absence of dragons.

Strange, he mused. *Not only dragons.* Nothing at all flew or crawled here. The only sign of life he observed were tiny fish swimming inside a clear pool. He watched these school around, darting from one end to the other. Smaller volcanic rocks rested beneath the pool.

Defeated, Kado climbed atop a boulder and sighed. *I wasted a trip,* he realized. *There are no dragons, it was only a story!*

Anger built inside the child, a tantrum of frustration and impatience that grew until he could no longer hold it in.

"I *needed* your help!" he shouted upward, accusing the heavens themselves. "I can't fight Lars without you!" he lamented. "You were supposed to be wise and mighty! I *needed* you to be real!"

The boy's thoughts turned to his mother and how she had left him, Briaca, and Father alone. It was her fault he was here, hers and that stupid Argant the Storyteller.

"Argant the Teller of Lies!" he screamed upward to no one.

Even Father did not know why his wife had left them, sneaking out in the night and leaving her husband and children to awaken to a morning filled with neither warmth nor love. They had needed her, all of them, but she selfishly left without reason or warning.

"What was so important, Mother, that you no longer loved us enough to stay?" he demanded from the heavens. "Everything changed! Father grew melancholy and forgot how to have fun. He came home every evening and picked up his whisky bottle instead of us. Even Briaca changed—mean and bossy without smiles, winks, or laughs! You ruined us, tore apart our family, leaving behind only those lies! I *hate* your lies, especially those you told about Erwan the Bold!"

Kado put everything he had into his anger. All those years of resentment, long repressed by love and hopeful thoughts of her return, surged into this outpouring and he screamed hatred. Finally, exhaustion won out over grief and rage. He gave in to the tears, sobbing his childhood into the crook of his arm.

Eventually, slumber overwhelmed the boy, too wretched for anything except dreams. In these dreams he found his mother.

Oksana stole a glance at her sleeping children then returned to knitting. Kado had fallen asleep first, his day so full of activity he could not handle any more. Briaca had resisted, her stubbornness so much like her father's, but eventually drifted off.

"They're getting too big for me to chase around and wrestle," Conrad said from his chair. Though his eyes were closed her husband would try not to sleep until she too had gone off to bed. "I think I pulled something in my back," he added with a smile. He loved his children dearly, as much as he loved his wife.

"You came home late," she pointed out, finally addressing the irritation she had hidden from the children. "What grim news do you bring?" she demanded.

"One of Lord Eduard's men called us away from our labor. A king's man addressed all of us in Cardac."

Oksana stiffened. Grim news indeed, for a king's man to call a meeting. "One of Chilperic's men? Who are we warring against now?" she demanded.

"He was vague, saying we were threatened by a *Roman threat*, but said nothing more."

"The real threat is here, in the kingdom, and it wears Eduard's clothing! He does the work of these Romans!" she snapped, her disdain for their sovereign's lineage unbridled. He was not a Gaul like her husband, the king's line spurred from the Romans, a patsy to their empire. "We grow poorer" she complained, "while he fattens from *our* labor!"

"I think that explains the threat," Conrad said, echoing the thoughts of other men in the town. Some of us believe there's finally been a revolt, he's risen against the Romans and joined the Franks north of Aventicum."

"And he'll waste every one of *you* until the empire quells it!" she added scornfully. "This *isn't* your fight!"

"No, but I won't be able to refuse once they stop taking volunteers. Soon they'll impress those who hold back. At least by joining up now I'll be trained in a specialty."

"A specialty?" she demanded. "Like waiving a pike around on the front lines?"

Conrad flinched but did not answer.

Oksana regretted her words at once. He was a brave man, but fear lurked beneath his calmness. He needed to believe he could survive better with a pike in his hands than with a pitchfork. "When King Chilperic is finished, all weapons will lay discarded upon the battlefield," she snapped. "I'm sorry," she told him. "Why don't you wash up and go to bed. I've some things to finish before I can join you."

Conrad stood, bending to kiss the top of her head before removing his boots from the hearth. "Don't stay up late," he begged his wife. "I won't be able to sleep until you're beside me."

"I know," she said through a feigned smile, "and I won't. I promise I'll be right behind you." Oksana waited until the bedroom door shut before throwing down her knitting. Only then did the tears fall, a blend of sorrow and anger toward the king.

A soft rap at the door dried them as quickly as they had started. There was no telling who had business at this hour. Jumping to her feet she eyed the bedroom door. Conrad should answer, but he needed rest more than she. With discernment enough to look out the peephole, she spied Argant the Storyteller standing in the moonlight outside.

Without hesitation Oksana opened the door and stepped out to join him.

"It's begun," he told her.

"Just as you foretold," she agreed.

"Just as you once made a pledge to give aid," he reminded the woman.

"I was a child then, no older than Kado."

"It's the only way," the old man said without flinching. His eyes drilled into hers, searching for a single waver in her resolve.

"But if Conrad goes away to fight, the children will need me!"

"*When* he goes away to fight, you and the children will answer to your own fates and he will return home to empty beds and a lonely hearth. Only *you* can do this!"

Oksana turned back toward the house, stared at the closed door, and imagined her family sleeping safely in their beds beyond the oaken boards. "I really don't have a choice, do I?" she asked in a quivering voice.

"No," the old man agreed, "you do not. Your pledge was the condition by which this life of yours was allowed. Now you must go, to be there when he blows the horn."

"Let me first get my things," she begged, reaching for the door.

"No!" Argant snapped. "I will not allow you to look upon their sleeping faces, one glance would be enough to break your oath! You leave now!"

Oksana nodded, her eyes filled with sadness and loss, then followed the Ancient One into the forest without looking back. Her body would never return, despite her heart remained with her family.

Kado awoke with a start, with his heart pounding in his ears and his mouth screaming, "Mother come back!"

He looked around, finding his surroundings unchanged, except for the darkness of night which had settled while he slumbered. The black rocks sat unmoving beside the crystal clear pool.

Now you must go, to be there when he blows the horn, the ghostly voice of Argant echoed in his awakened mind, speaking to the boy's mother in dream world.

He means me, Kado realized, *but I do not have a horn to blow!* He only had his satchel, the sparse bit of food remaining inside, his dagger, and the dragon's tooth.

An idea struck him, shaking his insides awake as violently as his mind had awakened, and he reached into the satchel to draw out the yellowed object. Its hollowness *did* resemble a horn, with its perfectly placed cavity on the tip of the fang.

Closing his eyes, the boy placed it to his lips and blew.

Chapter Ten

Kado blew out long and slow into the tooth, his breath becoming a deep, rumbling note that resonated through the valley. As he drew back his lips he listened. A sweet echo met his ears, at first the sound of a trumpet, but that changed as it subsided. The final tone before dissipating resembled a dragon's roar.

The boy raised the horn to his lips to create the sound a second time.

"So, you're cleverer than we hoped," the voice of Argant the Storyteller chuckled from the trees nearby.

The boy turned, his awe at the sound now lost, replaced by anger at the old man's sudden appearance in the night. "*You* made Mother go away!" he accused.

Argant paused only for a moment, his feet missing only the slightest of steps, and his eyes betrayed the briefest moment of uncertainty. He quickly recovered, ignoring the boy's accusation. "I must admit, there were those among us who believed you would never figure out the horn."

"I'm *not* a simpleton," Kado pointed out, "and don't change the subject. Where did you take my mother?"

"How are you so sure I had something to do with her leaving?" the old man countered. "Perhaps she had grown weary of child rearing, eager to return to a life where only *she* mattered? Or, perhaps your father was more violent than you remember and drove her away with fists and awful words?"

"No. I dreamt of her leaving with you..."

"What is a dream?" Argant cut him off, his voice booming into the valley as deeply resonant as the dragon's horn. "Is it not the concoction of the mind? A fabrication of the subconscious? Aren't dreams the lies of wanton fears?"

Kado recoiled from the angry roar, suddenly small when pinned beneath the man's grandeur. "It didn't feel like a dream," he whispered in defense.

"But you just said it was," the old man accused, his voice once again resembling a man's more than a god's. "What do *you* know about *anything,* child?" he asked with a shrug, as if he had no care for the boy at all.

"Nuh... nothing," Kado stammered. "I guess it was only a dream."

"He is too weak, Ancient One," a massive voice suggested, the tone of it a pleasant bass that shook the boy's chest.

Kado turned, finding several dragons standing where there had once been rocks. Each stood several strides high, at least twice that of a destrier.

There were so many shapes and sizes assembled before the boy. The smaller type walked on two legs and had shorter bodies, their arms stretching back and becoming wings. The chests on these were wide and muscular, and their faces seethed with anger at the human in their midst. The larger form, whom he guessed were the elders by the quiet calm on their faces, each walked on four broad and powerful legs. Their bodies were stockier than all the others, round and full, with wings far wider and grander than their smaller counterparts.

The boy scanned each and every one, taking in their broad assortment of colors. None among them appeared to be what he sought, the aerouants his mother had described as their fiercest warriors. Those would be serpentine, with elongated bodies snaking behind them, and with wide wings nearly as long as their bodies.

This assemblage was not at all what Kado imagined, and he marveled at their differences. Staring into the eyes of the speaker he quickly realized they all shared only one trait among the gathered species. Every pair of eyes burned red like fire, swirling and hypnotic, and impossible from which to look away.

"But he was chosen nonetheless," Argant argued, completely unbothered by the fact he conversed with a dragon, "and thus you must honor the bond."

The beast recoiled suddenly, so abruptly a rush of hot wind brushed against the boy's cheek. The dragon looked around, then pressed its steaming nostrils against Argant's chest. "I see no others of importance ready to stand with this child! He has not the heart of a warrior, nor does he deserve a protector!"

"I *am* a warrior!" Kado screamed defiantly. "I only need one of *you* to come along and help me take down Lars!"

The other dragons all laughed in unison, a rumbling sound that sputtered on the edges with sparks and undertones of crackling flame. All at once the beasts flew up into the air, their massive wings pushing so much of it aside that Kado was knocked to the ground. Even Argant had to shift his weight, holding an arm across his eyes to protect them from scattered dust and debris.

"You will have none of *us* to lend you aid," the dragons replied with a single voice, turning their backs in the air before lumbering off into the moonlight, seeking the distant horizon.

The parlay had ended.

"That's it?" Kado demanded, screaming after them. "Come back! I *am* a warrior! I've faced voltur!" As they retreated he grew deflated and weakly added with a whimper, "I *am* a warrior!"

"It's no use," the old man replied with a shrug. "They will not aid you no matter what else you shout. They've moved on to another place and will not return to Mount Sapientia until the stench of man has left their home."

"Wasted," Kado whispered. "My entire trip was wasted."

"Perhaps not," the old man said with a shrug but also turned his back to the boy, disappearing into the trees and leaving him alone.

Kado returned his eyes to the massive dragons, now mere specks against the bright moon above. *They would not even listen,* he thought angrily, a rush of hopelessness filling his heart. He had come all this way for nothing, not even finding live dragons was enough to restore his earlier ambition—knowing they existed only made his failure sting that much more.

A soft chittering and rhythmic clicking returned his attention to the valley. All of the massive boulders were gone, but so too were the smaller rocks in the pool. The water no longer sat still and unmoving, but rippled from disruption. Along its edge stood a dozen lizards, each the size of Kado's forearm. They shook water from their backs.

Kado's eyes grew round with curiosity, watching the tiny beasts and wondering what they were. There was no way these were dragons, their elongated bodies made them look more like snakes with tiny wings and stubby legs. *Although...* Their heads were the same shape as those larger creatures, rounded and full, with large eyes that swam dizzyingly like fire with their inner heat.

"What are you?" the boy asked the creatures. "You're not dragons."

They did not answer, only watched and inclined their heads at his question. They, unlike their larger cousins, did not seem to understand him.

"Now!" a raspy voice whispered from the trees. Two shapes darted out, lunging for the tiny creatures.

"Stop!" Kado shouted, recognizing at once the voltur from the previous night. Instinctively he reached into his satchel and drew out the dagger, then watched with horror as the monsters each scooped up one of the tiny lizards, fangs bared and piercing the scaly underside of soft bellies.

The lizard creatures writhed and squealed, caught and dying as the voltur drank. Their brothers and sisters scrambled to move behind Kado, seeking his protection from the newcomers' thirst.

The boy had frozen, holding his small dagger in front of his trembling body.

Having sucked the entire lifeforce from their meal, both voltur wiped their mouths and tossed the drained carcasses aside. Turning toward Kado with insatiable thirst, they grinned crimson teeth.

Chapter Eleven

The voltur smiled at Kado with gruesome intent. Too weak and pathetic to fight back, the boy would provide their next meal. Behind him the tiny lizards cowered, ill-fated by placing their hope of survival in the child. Held forward, his tiny dagger wavered with fear.

"Thank you, boy," one of the vile creatures purred, "for bringing us here!"

"Yes," added the other. "Leaving him alive to lead us was a good idea."

"Now give us the others," the first voltur commanded, "and we *might* let you live."

Kado considered its words. *They might let me flee, but they won't allow me to live. I've seen them, heard them speak, and for that alone I will become a meal.*

"Step aside!" the other growled. "Leave us to our decadence."

Both sets of voltur lips smacked at the thought of feasting on the lizards, and one of them nicked its lip on a fang. A grey tongue licked the trail of oozing blood.

Kado briefly looked down at the lizards, weaker and more pathetic than him. With defiance he raised his eyes and told the voltur, "No."

Both creatures laughed then lunged.

Kado's knife flashed as if it had a mind of its own, slicing the air. The boy, shocked by his instinctual movement, watched the monsters recoil. "I'll take at least one of you with me!" he promised.

"No matter," the first of them said, shrugging off his refusal with a laugh. "Because of you we've learned the way up the cliffs and will feast on dragon blood with all our kin."

As quickly as they had arrived, they were off again. Tree branches rustled as they disappeared once more into the forest.

Kado looked down at the lizards, now rubbing against his legs like hungry kittens. "Don't worry," he assured them, "your parents will be back soon to protect you, that's what parents do is protect their young." Thinking about his own, his voice cracked a bit at the end. His weren't coming back either.

With that, the creatures scampered off into the pool, breaking its glasslike surface and diving down to the sandy bottom. They again curled as if sleeping, once more taking the appearance of volcanic rocks.

Kado felt relieved. Had they remained he would have been beholden to protect them from the voltur should any return. Now he could flee in the same manner, returning to the warmth of his own bed in the home of his sister.

Only... he remembered, *Briaca's not there!* Lars had her enslaved, along with most of Cardac. *But what can I do?* he asked himself. *I'm just a boy without even a dragon.*

"Aerouants," a voice corrected from behind. Argant the Storyteller had returned. "You wanted to bond with an aerouant, yet here you are, too blind to appreciate the gift one has given you."

"I've bonded nothing," Kado argued, pointing the way the dragons had gone. "They all rejected me, leaving me behind to fight off the voltur. I... I couldn't even do *that* properly!"

"Hmm," the old man pondered. "To me it appeared you defended dragons."

"Not at all," Kado disagreed, pointing to the drained carcasses by the water's edge. "When the dragons return they will blame *me* for those deaths."

"Why would they blame you?" Argant demanded with a frown.

"Because I led the voltur here. It's my fault the dragon children are dead."

Argant laughed so loudly the entire valley boomed with his glee, an odd response to such dire news.

"What's so funny, old man?" Kado challenged, bowing up for a fight. He would beat this storyteller with his fists if he thought it would teach the old man a lesson. "It seems you've been laughing at me this entire time!"

"Children? You think the aerouants are *children*? You, Kado, son of Conrad, alone suffer the ignorance of childhood. Those," he said pointing at the pool, "are not the dragon's young. They are their *warriors*! They protect the elders! All of these are in *second* form!"

The boy froze, gazing at the bottom of the pool with confusion clouding his face. That idea was impossible, so far-fetched to believe those little lizards could be warriors much less the protectors of such grand and powerful dragons.

Then it was Kado's turn to laugh. It came out at first as a chuckle, then grew into delirium. That laughter turned to anger. The boy's eyes narrowed as he cackled and shook his head in disgust. "You're a fool," he said, "and so I name you Argant the *Idiot*."

The old man shrugged. "So I've been accused." He pointed over Kado's shoulder and observed, "But it seems one has chosen you."

The boy turned to look, praying one of the massive dragons had returned. That feeling of hope escaped with a single sigh, as he found the smallest of the lizards stood on its hind legs with what could have been called a smile on its oddly shaped face. Its huge eyes swam like those of the elder, burning embers of fire that reflected a pitiful child determined to exact his revenge.

"Go away," Kado told it, but it only chittered and swayed as if its large head would topple its elongated body to the ground. Somehow it remained upright. The boy turned, about to tell the storyteller he didn't want the stupid lizard, but the old man had once more practiced his annoying habit of disappearing at the most ill-timed moments. "I don't want it!" he yelled toward the forest, the gentle swaying of branches his only answer.

The lizard moved closer, rubbing against the boy's feet.

"Stop that," he said, but the lizard only pressed harder. "I said, stop!" he shouted, giving it a gentle kick toward the pond. Instead of darting into the pool to rejoin the others, it redoubled its efforts and scurried over to rub his legs once more.

"One more thing," the storyteller's voice announced, the old man's head reemerging from behind broad leaves. "After making your way down the rock face, you'll want to be moving due east."

Kado let his heart settle after the fright from Argant's sudden arrival, then asked, "Why would I go east? Cardac and Lars are north."

"You *could* go try and kill Lars with your pathetic little dagger, but you want to go east."

"Why, old man?"

"Because that pair of voltur will reach their legion by tomorrow night, so you have to find them and kill them before they make it there and warn their friends."

"I've no problem with them heading the opposite way of me," Kado argued. "I'm going after Lars."

The old man shrugged. "Okay," he said, "suit yourself." He turned to leave, the branches snapping in place between him and the boy. Over his shoulder he added, "But if you let them reach their legion they'll return and feast until no dragon exists on this mountain. But fine, return north if you don't want to know why your mother left with me in the middle of the night."

Kado ran after the storyteller, pulling aside the broad leaves and finding nothing but forest on the other side. Argant had done it again, disappeared at the most annoying time. *So it's true,* he thought, *and that wasn't a dream when I saw her leave!* He gave the little aerouant one more kick to send it tumbling toward the pool, then darted into the forest. It was time to return home.

Chapter Twelve

Kado eyed the way down, a much more treacherous descent than it had been as a climb. He wavered, fearful of losing his footing—a surety since he could not help but look down. He glanced toward the clearing in the center of the crater. If only one of the real dragons had chosen him instead of that pesky lizard, he could have ridden its back all the way to Cardac just like Erwan the Bold.

Stupid lizards, he thought, cursing Argant's joke. *There's no way those are the aerouants, the protectors of dragons!*

He drew a deep breath and let it escape slowly, ready to make his way down the mountain. His left foot stepped forward, finding footing while his eyes locked firmly on the path. The rest of the world blurred, almost daring him to divert his eyes and look upon the deadlier way down. After a while he found a rhythm and breathed more easily.

Something darted past his foot just as he set it down, nearly losing balance. Kado cursed again. It was the lizard, rushing by and leaping to the next set of rocks that made him stumble. He grabbed the nearest crevice, hugging the cold stone now dripping wet with melting ice and snow.

"Blaze you!" the boy muttered between panting breaths. "I told you to stay!"

Slowly he lifted his head from the rocks, turning to look at the creature. It sat ten paces away, standing on hind legs and watching him dubiously. Its head cocked as if reasoning out his anger.

"What are *you* looking at?" Kado demanded. "I don't want *you!* I want a real dragon, not a pathetic, weak thing like *you!*"

The stubborn creature merely stared up at the boy.

"Don't you understand me?" The big dragons had, the eldest had even spoken to him without any difference in language. Why wouldn't this little one understand? "Leave me!"

The tiny thing astonished him, slowly shaking its head back and forth as if saying, *No.* Then it raised a tiny arm, pointing a single claw downward before scurrying down the next ledge. There it watched and waited as if urging Kado to follow.

Slowly and carefully, the boy did.

Thankfully, the rocks were less icy the closer he came to the bottom of the cliff. Though wet, his father's boots found traction. The only trouble spot was the part that had broken away, but he made it across using the same handhold and cubby as before, reversing the process. After that he moved faster, keeping his eyes on the creature leaping and hopping several paces ahead. It almost felt as if it were showing him the best places to step. Reaching the bottom felt like an eternity, but the pair made it with a final jump.

Kado set off immediately north toward Cardac. *I'll kill him with my hands,* he decided, thinking of Lars. *Or my knife. I'll wait till he's asleep and sneak in and kill him in his bed. Then I'll find and free Briaca. She'll help me free the others!*

Something hit him hard against the back of his knee, folding his weight backward and knocking the boy to the ground. Fearing the voltur had arrived, he quickly rolled. Resting on his heels with fists up ready to fight, he looked around. There was no threat, only an angry, hissing aerouant.

The tiny creature stood on hind legs with mouth open in a pitiful roar. Instead of a bellowing threat, it came out as a squeaking hiss. Kado noticed its tiny wings fanned out to make itself appear bigger.

"What do you *want?*" Kado demanded. "Why can't you talk? You're useless to me, worthless!"

The creature turned eastward, sending out a single puff of smoke that trailed off in that direction.

"I don't understand you!" the boy screamed. "Cardac is *this* way," he said, pointing north. "The dragons won't help me, the aerouants are useless, so I'm going home to kill Lars!" He jumped to his feet, turning his back on the creature. He started to run toward the forest, eager to make up for a wasted day and night and put this nightmare of disappointment behind him.

Once again something struck the back of his knee, this time with more force.

Kado not only fell, he landed hard on his hands, his right wrist surging with pain. With tears in his eyes he rolled over, roaring anger up at the bright blue sky peaking above the treetops. If the gods lived there, they had ignored this boy's need for revenge.

Doubt suddenly won. Who was this child to stand up to such a villain as Lars? With only a steel knife and a dragon tooth, he was no match for the warlord and all his thugs. Tears streamed down his cheeks as he sobbed out any bravery he once held inside.

The lizard jumped on his chest and stared into his face, hot breath against the boy's nose, drying his tears into puffs of steam. Its eyes swirled as if ablaze, angry and dangerously focused on Kado's.

"Voltur," it finally managed, whispering in a soft, barely audible voice. The steamy word burned the boy's nose.

Kado remembered Argant's warning. If the voltur were allowed to reach their legion, none of the dragons would be safe. "I can't fight them," he told the lizard. "They'll devour us both if we try."

"Voltur," the aerouant said again. "Kill them."

The boy shook his head rapidly. "I don't know how," he lied. Fearful and finally honest with himself, he admitted the worst. "I'm a coward. I can't do *any* of this! I can't face those monsters again! I can't even stop Lars!"

The aerouant abruptly leapt to the ground, racing several paces toward the east. Then it stopped and spun around. "I help," it said, waiting for the boy to follow.

"How?" Kado asked between sobs, sitting up and hugging his knees. "You're just like me, small and useless." Then he realized the little creature had really spoken. Not once, but twice, it had managed real words, nearly stringing together sentences. The boy blabbered so many questions at once. "How will you help?" he demanded. "How much can you say? What if they see us coming?"

"I help," it said again, walking away toward the east.

Emboldened, Kado wiped away his tears and followed. Together, they started toward the voltur legion.

Filled with so many more questions, they poured forth in a torrent. But the aerouant never answered any of them, only led the boy further eastward into the forest. As nighttime neared, the pair reached a wide riverbank. There, the creature abruptly spun around and spoke. "Kill them now," it said quietly, a sentence fully formed, "before they awaken."

"I..." Kado stammered. "I don't understand. How? Where are they?" His eyes darted every direction, only seeing the rushing water, sharp rocks, and more forest beyond.

The aerouant turned south, toward the mountain range, and followed the riverbank without answering.

"How?" the boy again demanded. He was losing his patience with the small creature, despite its newfound ability to speak. Doubt returned with each step, creeping in and daring him to run away to Cardac. Just as he was about to give up, the pair emerged from the trees and stood beneath another tall cliffside.

High overhead a river cascaded over the side, falling as a wall of water into a pond below. Kado stared up with wonder. He had never imagined such a beautiful sight and, as far as he knew, no one from his village had ever mentioned this place. He would have remembered if they had.

The aerouant raced along the bank toward the cliffside, then abruptly disappeared.

"Where did you go?" Kado gasped. He hurried forward, reaching the cliff and looking left and right for the creature.

It had vanished.

After several moments it reappeared, emerging from beneath the waterfall and shaking off its icy spray. Beneath its feet the boy noticed a small ledge, narrower than the path he had followed up the mountain. The aerouant turned and showed him a passage.

Kado followed, squeezing between the water and the rocks, side-stepping until he stood dripping in a cavern. It took several minutes for his eyes to adjust to the shadows, and he spent the time hugging himself for warmth and rubbing feeling into his arms and legs. If he did not light a fire soon he may die from the cold.

As if on cue, the aerouant coughed and sputtered, then spit tiny sparks onto a nest of kindling on the cavern floor. The resulting flame lit the room and revealed voltur hiding against the rocks.

Chapter Thirteen

Kado recoiled the moment he saw the voltur. There were two. He was unsure if these were the same as those he had run into before, but they did resemble them very closely. Their spindly arms clutched rounded stomachs, still full of their bloody breakfast. Both sets of eyes clenched tightly shut, their lips curled in matching grimaces, pain wracking each from within. Bared fangs seemed to smile at the boy from their sleep. He watched the monsters closely to be sure, but they appeared to be deeply sleeping off their meal.

"Hurry," a whispered, human voice urged from behind.

Kado spun around to find Argant had joined him.

"You must kill them now while they're weakest, before they awaken with renewed strength, empowered by dragon sanguis."

Too afraid to be shocked by the storyteller's arrival, the boy pulled the tiny knife from his satchel and inched closer to the sleeping voltur.

"No," the old man warned, "not with that."

"It's all I have," Kado gave hushed argument, he would do the deed and be done with it.

"You have the only tool you need. An aerouant's bite will kill them."

The boy glanced sideways at the watching creature, its sharp teeth mere needles incapable of killing these beasts. It seemed unwilling or unable to step forward to help as promised. It shook its head as if to agree with the futility of the notion.

Kado raised the knife high above the first voltur, bringing it down quickly with enough force to pierce the heart. To his astonishment the blade shattered into pieces, unable to break the skin no matter how thin it looked. His eyes grew wide, staring into the shocked, open eyes of the awakened monster.

The voltur hissed, clutching the back of Kado's neck with sharp claws that drew the boy's blood. Though it struggled, the monster pulled his meal closer to its fangs, digging in its nails and using all the strength it could muster.

"The dragon's tooth!" Argant urged. "Use it now!"

Kado used one hand to push hard against the creature's chest, losing the battle as the rancid breath grew nearer. With his other he reached into the satchel, rooting around blindly until it grasped bone. Using all his strength he brought it upward, driving it deep beneath the voltur's ribs.

The monster gasped and its eyes grew glassy, its dying strength failing after a desperate attempt to feed from the boy. The voltur collapsed in a heap.

"Good," Argant praised quietly, "and now the other!"

It still slept, oblivious to the ruckus mere inches away.

Kado's hands now flashed with certainty, unafraid and filled with rage. With a single motion they slammed the dragon's tooth into the voltur's chest. He watched its eyes open wide with confusion, turning in unison to focus on the boy.

"Goro... will... prevail!" it promised before dying.

"It took him long enough!" Argant exclaimed to the aerouant, throwing his arms up in frustration. "I thought he'd *never* figure it out! I said *only an aerouant's bite will kill them,* but did he listen?" The tiny creature shook its head sharply. "That's right! I had to spell it out to him! *Use the tooth!* I said. I might as well have drawn him a picture and given him colored wax to fill in the lines." The old man shook his head, calmed his voice, then added, "He's not slow, only cautious, this one, but hesitation will be his downfall if he can't find the fire within!" The aerouant nodded and joined the old man beside the fire.

"What if I hadn't figured out your riddles at all?" Kado demanded, his fear replaced by anger. "They would have killed me!"

"*Pssh*," the old man dismissed his worry. "Your aerouant would have protected you."

The boy stole a glance at the creature, now sleeping in a curled ball at the storyteller's feet. He doubted it would have been much use at all. "Why did you choose now to return?" he asked.

"Because I realized I haven't finished telling the story of Erwan the Bold."

"I know the tale. Erwan bonded his aerouant and flew down from the mountain, returning to Aventicum, the capital city, and defeated the Roman army. Then he killed Dominus Titus."

"Okay then, you already know it all," the old man decided, jumping suddenly to his feet with surprising agility. "I'll be off, then."

"Wait!"

"But you already *know* it!"

"I..." Kado paused. Why *had* he interrupted? Then he realized. This story was all he had left of his mother, their deepest connection, and hearing it brought back all these recent memories of her. "I *want* to hear it," he admitted. "I *need* to hear it, I just wish it was from her lips, not yours."

"You miss her," Argant agreed with a nod.

The boy looked up from the flames, meeting the eyes of both storyteller and aerouant. The tiny creature almost seemed to be crying. Tiny drops of steam sizzled on its snout. "Of course I do. She never should have left us. Why did you lead her away?"

The old man shrugged. "She had something she had to do, an act of great sacrifice the likes of which legends are told."

"Will she ever return?" he asked. "*Can* she return?"

Kado waited as Argant considered his response. Even the aerouant stared up expectantly. "Your mother, as you knew her, no longer exists."

A lump filled Kado's throat, choking back his next words.

Sensing the boy's sadness, the storyteller resumed the tale. "Erwan the Bold had awakened before sunrise, appraising the cliffside and deciding if he should climb. Now, this was a different time of year than when you arrived. Spring, if I remember correctly, but the result was the same. As the sun rose above the horizon the path was briefly revealed. There is a narrow window for this phenomenon, as the dragons intended when they carved it, many millennia ago.

"They knew the voltur would try and find it but also knew the creatures only ventured out at night, darting to the safety of their caves long before first light can catch them exposed. They're not full vampure and so they can't walk in the light as easily. It burns them, weakens them immensely, hence why they did not fight you for the other aerouants. They hadn't the strength after following you up the cliff in daylight. If they had tried, your steel might have harmed them."

"What about the dominus, the one who sucked the life from Erwan's wife and children?" Kado asked. "How did *he* walk in daylight?"

"Remember I told you he had an ailment? One that required human blood?"

"Yes. You called it *sanguis*."

"Hmmm, so I did..." The old man considered the word, almost seeing it in his mind before continuing. "Sanguis is more than blood though, it contains the lifeforce of whatever living thing it resides in."

"Like ichor?" the boy asked, using the term for the lifeforce of the gods.

"Similar, but only by the broadest of stretch. Sanguis is the physical form of a soul. It resides within the blood and makes you Kado instead of Briaca or Lars." He spat when he spoke the latter. "No, Titus the Abominable was a vampure, a creature worse than a voltur because he could walk in the light, appearing as a normal human in every way imaginable. The only difference was that he must consume sanguis to survive."

"But you said Titus was mortal. I thought vampure and voltur live forever."

"He was mortal, all vampure are..." Argant trailed off as if thinking of some horrible image then quickly recovered, "until they consume the sanguis of dragonkind."

"Dragon*kind*? You mean like all those I saw? The different forms including the aerouants?"

"Yes, those are the versions you have seen, but rest assured there are more you have not encountered."

"And all of them share this sanguis, the soul which the vampure crave?"

"Most certainly. Dragon sanguis gifts them immortality. Those you met this morning are descended from an Elderkin, he's older than time itself, just as the vampure are descended from a single source."

"Elderkin?"

"The largest among them, the four-footed type with broader body, he who ignored your pleas is called Dregal."

Kado nodded, remembering the nobility the form conveyed.

"The original Elderkin flew the skies long before humans walked upon the ground, and his descendants can live forever as long as their lives are not interrupted. The vampure crave that blessing and yearn for the sanguis he passed on to his offspring."

"So King Titus had never consumed dragon sanguis? Is that why you said he was mortal?"

"At the time he devoured Erwan's family, no. He was quite mortal at the time, a wretched creature addicted to human sanguis—too much so to bother seeking out dragonkind. He drank from any opportunity he could find and had many peasants to choose from."

"What happened next in the story?" Kado asked quietly. "What did Erwan find atop Mount Sapientia?"

"He found the same dragons as you. Even Dregal was there, but he was a fully formed aerouant at the time. They all gathered, conversed, and listened to his plea. Because the vampure are their ancient enemy, one agreed to aid him on his quest. The largest, most ancient aerouant of them all carried Erwan to Aventicum, just as you said. From there his story became legend, he battled Titus, who was defeated."

"Why did Erwan never make himself king?" the boy asked. "He had dragons, he could have ruled the world."

"Because dragonkind do not share human ambitions and will not aid a self-righteous endeavor."

Kado considered this. "That's why they flew away from *me*," he realized. "I seek vengeance, and that's self-righteous."

The storyteller nodded. "I set you up for that, stirring the anger within you, but it was for a reason. The dragons had to judged your passion for themselves, to see your motives as true vengeance or a selfless act." He gestured toward the aerouant again sleeping at his feet. "This little one recognized your heart is pure, that you also seek to free your sister and the rest of your village from a tyrant, and so she has chosen you to be her vinculum."

"She's a girl?" Kado felt a bit disappointed.

"She is, and has led you on your first quest as her vinculum. I'm happy to say you passed your first test."

Kado turned his gaze to the bodies now rotting in the corner of the cave. "By killing these voltur have I redeemed myself after leading them to Sapientia? They can no longer tell their legion how to scale the cliffs, so I can finally face Lars?"

"No, not completely, but it was a good start. You still have much to do, including killing the others in their legion. They will come looking for their kin and, when they do, they will blame your village."

Kado nodded, swallowing down a lump. "I know how to kill them now," he realized. "I only have to find them while they are sleeping like these were."

"Yes, and this time you will have more help from your little friend." Argant waved his hand and Kado suddenly felt sleepiness overcome him. "For now, rest, dream truth, and awaken refreshed for your journey."

Kado yawned and stretched, unable to resist the feeling passing through his mind and body. Without another thought he slept.

Chapter Fourteen

Conrad held his pike at the ready, level with left hand forward with the weight of it controlled in his right. He was in the middle of the block, third row, fourth man in. Over three sets of shoulders he could see the enemy pikes bobbing in the air. They advanced with determination.

"Pikemen… Push!" King Chilperic commanded from his steed, determined to be an inspiration for his troops. His arm, no longer bound in a sling, gripped a sword. His leg had healed slower, splinted and free of its stirrup. Conrad had watched a host of pages and squires literally lash the knight to his destrier at his insistence. The sovereign would ride into victory, this final battle determining the fate of the Gaulish realm.

Conrad moved with the block, his body squeezed from all sides as his feet moved in step with the cadence caller. *Hut… hut… hut… hut…*, the rhythm beat in his mind, marked by each step.

"Draw!" Chilperic cried, and the front line drew swords.

Without another warning, Conrad felt the weight of three dozen men crash against the enemy block of another three dozen. They were perfectly matched.

Warm wetness splashed across his face as swords sliced. His ears listened to moans and grunts as blades stabbed. Abruptly the man ahead of him drew and stepped forward. Conrad filled in the second row, feeling the body of another pikeman fill in behind him.

Despite the death all around, the battle must be going well. "Keep pushing, men!" Chilperic urged. "We have the field!"

Abruptly, thunderous hooves sounded from the left flank. Enemy cavalry rushed down, quickly gaining advantage. Conrad stole another glance at Chilperic. He too had noticed the change of fate, but did so too late. An arrow took him through the neck, the impact knocking him limp upon his mount. As the horse bucked and kicked, the body of the king flapped as uselessly in the air as his banner.

That was not good for the Gaulish army but especially the pikemen. Neither the death of their king or the flanking charge bode well their chances. Though designed to fight cavalry head on, a sideways attack would scatter and route the block. They must remain united at all costs. With no time to mourn, Conrad peeled his eyes away from fallen king and focused on the fight in front of him, watching as an enemy sword dropped the front man.

"Push!" a commanding voice bellowed, as a group of knights raced toward the breaking lines. The banner waving over this Frankish nobleman, a blue field with three straw colored toads, belonged to Clovis, from one of the northern kingdoms. A host of light cavalry raced after their king, each adorned in his heraldry.

Conrad drew his blade and rushed forward just as armored cavalry trampled the middle rows, including where he had just stood. A sword swung at him, giving him no time to look behind him. With no body pressed against his, he feared the worst—Conrad had no replacement should he fall.

Kado suddenly felt himself flying over the battlefield, no longer seeing the world from his father's perspective but from another, sadder set of eyes. Though he could not explain how, he knew he now existed as that elder who had spoken on Mount Sapientia. With angry eyes he scanned the ground as Dregal, his vision sharper than an entire flock of eagles.

The left flank of the Romans had crumbled, leaving it vulnerable to a second infantry charge from the Franks. He watched as two light cavalry filled in where the pikemen had fallen, using their animals' breasts to knock sword and shield aside. Far below, King Clovis' brigade raced to move more pikeman blocks to cover the gap, pulling from the last of the Gaulish reserves.

He felt oddly safe at this altitude, unafraid of falling or being spotted by archers on the ground. At this height he would resemble a bird or condor at worst and flew casually without worry. His only concern now was over the outcome of the battle. Should King Clovis win, he would secure all of Frankia, and soon Gaul, under his fluttering banners.

This battle would turn the tide for the rebellion in the region, expelling the Romans and their war-mongering emperor. These Latins had committed centuries to killing or pushing many dragonkind from their peninsula, as did the Hellenes from the eastern archipelago. The final effort resulted in a successful recapture of their flank, breaking the Romans and sending them into full retreat.

The world had changed since the onset of mankind; they had grown organized while dragonkind hid. Dregal sadly shook his broad head before turning toward home to Sapientia. He hoped the boy and the Ancient One had gone, taking that rebellious aerouant with them. She was foolish but insistent, that stubborn one and must have surely chosen the boy as her vinculum. He rued the day the Ancient One had allowed her to wander from the thunder, but it was her right to choose a path. As an aerouant, any she chose would expose her to danger.

Hopefully, both she and the Ancient One had chosen the vinculum well.

Interlude:
Erwan
the
Bold

Erwan the Bold

Read no further if you desire a romantic tale. What lies ahead is tragedy, a retelling of what was lost more than gained. This tome weaves a story about dragons, those ancient wyrms of which only legends remain—long after their bones have turned to dust.

Oh! But don't go too far, it is also a tale of vampires.

Forget immediately what you know about both these creatures, because legends and myths are merely lies. I bring to you the truth, a story passed down by generations but retold much differently than I now relate it to you.

What is this? You ask *who am I* to regale such a heart-wrenching tale, and to *change* it nonetheless?

I am Argant the Old, the Storyteller, the wise, and long-lived. I am also called the *Ancient One,* not only by gods and men, but also puca, sith, vampires, and dragons.

But why even tell a tragedy in the first place? Why not entertain you with a tale of love and conquest? Is not that thing, which humankind desires most, merely romance?

Oh, but it most certainly is not, not if a mind truly knows the world.

While it is true that audiences crave falsehoods, those glorified narratives of victory and love, they also yearn to terrify or distress depending upon their mood. But as far as mankind's interest in history goes, of which legends are but a splinter, these same audiences demand to be shielded from the truth. They seek joy even when their lives thrive on calamity. Humans merely use romance to fill their hearts with hope—knowing reality would terrify their souls.

Like sheep, the gullible cling to mummers' fabrications of happiness, attending dramatization without satisfying the true hunger within—the basal desire to feed on excitement. Happy endings leave the audience empty, always needing more, whereas tragedies nourish the soul. One can only stand to consume so much, until finding it has overflowed.

Trust old Argant when I tell you, the best stories tell of vengeance and loss, but never in that order.

So proceed if you must, but not without heeding a warning. Just as audiences crave fantastic wonders, the lustful creatures recounted in these pages require satiation. They must be given what they crave, untenable and unquenchable feasting. If left to hunger, their true nature rips free just as easily as sanguis rushes from their victim's veins.

All hereafter is a story about that feasting and how a single man satisfied his own lust for vengeance after involving himself in a war between dragons and vampires.

It begins, ironically, with a tale of romance...

Erwan meant nothing to the world before he met me. He was always a lamentable sham and a poorly born one at that! Those names I call him are titles earned from his earlier years, but he would become, after fate woefully changed his life, Erwan the Bold.

This version factually tells a more magnificent story than the man deserves. It is a saga befitting heroes of yore, great men and women who excelled in the face of adversity, who found greatness lurking within and discovered their lives were meant to soar the heavens!

Erwan's life, his entire existence, began and ended with dirt.

Dirt resided upon his mother's face and on the ground where the midwife knelt to catch and welcome his filthy entrance. His parents owned not even a bit of that dirt in and upon which they toiled. It clung, especially to that spot behind the ears and in crevices rarely washed, like Erwan, out of sight and mind.

That Erwan grew to work this same parcel as his parents had always been foretold. A son of a serf is nothing but another worker upon the nobleman's land, one to replace the father's eventual passing. He is tied to that land, bound to it, destined to die upon and be rested beneath it, just as his parents were once doomed to be entombed.

Fate had a plan involving the dirt Erwan worked, but he somehow defied that destiny.

Despite his poverty, Erwan enjoyed riches unobtainable by his Roman overseer, Dominus Titus the Abominable, the owner of the dirt which so entirely ruled Erwan's life. The peasant had found love, a wonderful thing for a lowly man of pitiful station, in the form of sweet Adelia. She was clean, free of the soil to which her future husband had always been bound. Erwan believed her perfectly angelic, sent to him by the gods. In truth, no one knew from where she travelled.

They met along the road to Cardac, a crucial point to mention in this story. Their meeting, an incidental moment made possible by random timing, unraveled the tightly wound threads of Erwan's fate.

Married in a quiet ceremony, the pair retreated to his allotted parcel of dirt and lived as man and wife. There she bore him two children, Rupert and Racinda, in the same fashion and poverty into which he himself was born. These children so loved their father and hurried each day to meet him along that road to Cardac. They greeted him each afternoon with hugs after his morning spent laboring for Dominus Titus.

Our story begins on the day they failed to meet him along the way.

Warm sunlight danced over the treetops. On this spring afternoon, filled with hopeful promise, Erwan's back ached. He had spent the entire day stooped or bent over, tending the fleshy seedlings reaching for blue skies above. This pain did not dampen his mood, not in the slightest. So much of life warmed his heart.

Erwan had tended the entire field in just a few days—backbreaking work with only his hoe and scythe to aid him. Thankful for the bounty it would bring the dominus, he prayed, not for a horse or a plow to make the work easier, but that this crop would turn out a good one, bountiful enough to pay both tax and tithe. His family would enjoy whatever grain was left over, and the bigger the yield the better it would serve them. He finished his prayer with a smile, thankful and hopeful in giving his words of praise.

So much in his world was exactly as it should be, and he would soon fill his belly with a meal prepared by Adelia. But first he would finish his walk, met along the way by Rupert and Racinda. On some days the twins would hop out of the woods and roar like bears, eager to send fright down their father's spine. He would cry out and cower, then laugh out loud at their joke. On others they would simply bowl him over, coming down the path in a foot race, the winner enjoying the first-prize hug.

He passed a broken trunk, a tree felled by lighting several years before. It was here they usually met up.

It's odd, he mused but did not worry. They would be along very soon.

With each step the father's concern grew into worry. Perhaps they had been held up by chores or had been playing so hard they lost track of time. Neither of those calamities had ever prevented their arrival before. He pondered their tardiness, hopeful but with optimism quickly souring.

Something is wrong, he realized, *or they would be here by now!*

His mind wandered, imagining the worst. Perhaps a bear had ambled from the forest, or a wolf! No, neither had dared come near his hovel for many years. Though they resided a good twenty minutes outside of Cardac, the smell of human kept both predators at bay.

Unless it's rabid, his mind taunted.

His pace quickened, a fast walk at first that grew into a full-fledged run. He must arrive home in time, no matter what problems waited. Nothing would harm his family as long as he...

He skidded to a halt, both feet kicking up dirt across the road.

Up ahead a carriage rested beside his hovel, a magnificent vehicle drawn by matching horses each as splendidly white as the other. The car itself had been painted a dark crimson that stood out against gilded edges reflecting golden sunlight. Even the wheels boasted of wealth, the likes of which Erwan had never imagined.

Who visits my home? he wondered, moving forward with trepidation, just as two swordsmen stepped out from behind the tiny building. Both men wore the colors and herald of Dominus Titus, the Roman overseer.

"You there, peasant!" one of the strangers commanded. "Drop your weapons and stay where you are!"

The sound of hoof beats stamped the dirt behind him, and Erwan found himself surrounded on all sides by Romans. "Who are you?" he demanded, eyeing the war destriers warily. They seemed more dangerous than the drawn blades in the footmen's hands.

"Never mind who we are," one of them said dismissively. "Lay down your weapons and return the way you came. Be gone from here!"

"But I..." Erwan stammered, perplexed by their commands. He had no weapons, only the tools of a farmer. "I live here!" he protested.

The two swordsmen exchanged a look. The shorter man shrugged to the other but said nothing. The taller man seemed to be in charge.

"Oh, the hell with him!" one of the mounted knights decided, his armored boot kicking forward and meeting Erwan's temple. The world around the farmer swam with dark spots as he thudded to the ground in a heap. His scythe and hoe landed nearby, discarded and forgotten.

Just as soon as he had landed another man appeared from within the hovel, wiping his mouth on a silken handkerchief. It was darkly smeared and smudged, soiled and therefore undignified for such an aristocrat to carry. This newcomer was obviously a nobleman by the fancy cut and quality of his cloth. He tossed the bit of cloth away while stepping through the doorway. The highborn noble winced uncomfortably at the sun now hanging low over the trees.

As Erwan's vision swam into focus he realized he had seen this man before, and that single moment had proven unforgettable. It was Dominus Titus the guest of the mayor whose feast had drawn the entire town the night before. This man bore blessings by the Roman Emperor himself.

The dominus held one hand over his eyes to hide the light. His bloodstained teeth showed clearly behind his scowl. "Deal with him," Titus commanded his knights. "I no longer desire a taste for blood." Without another word the nobleman stepped aboard his carriage, shutting himself away while the driver readied the horses.

Above Erwan, the world darkened as violent men blocked the sun. He cowered as the first blows landed, kicks, jabs, and punches, then plunged entirely into a world of blackness.

Hours later, Erwan opened both eyes, matted and encased beneath a coating of dried blood. This hurt less than the agony in his ribs, but he winced all the same. Every inch of his body would bruise, left for dead and discarded in the woods.

He tried three times to regain his feet, to stand and find his bearings, but fell twice back to earth with agonizing thuds. He was more careful on the third attempt, moving slower so that the spinning in his head would catch up to the throbbing of his limbs. When he could finally look around to survey his surroundings, he realized night had fallen.

At first Erwan felt lost in familiar woods, among trees he had grown up playing, but soon he found his bearings.

This old pine with the crooked trunk points north, he told himself, *and so home is this way.* Each step sent shockwaves through the farmer's ribs, but he never slowed until he reached the clearing around his hovel. What he saw made him break into a run.

Several creatures had gathered on his doorstep, each as gaunt as it was pale. Onward he ran despite pounding torment up his spine. Each step hurt worse than the last, but he ignored that pain, pushing it to the back of his mind. He had to reach his home.

One of the creatures turned, its bloodshot eyes surprised to see a man rushing forth. It rushed to meet him, moving faster than any human or animal the farmer had ever seen.

Erwan ducked as it came closer, just as he passed the place where Titus' men had beaten him. His tools still lay discarded where he dropped them, and he scooped up his scythe, grabbing the simple wooden handle with a callused hand.

The ghastly specter bared fangs as it ran, grinning a wild expectation of feast. Beyond it, two more had joined their comrade, rushing faster toward him than any human could run.

The farmer stepped to the side as the first arrived, squaring off to face it in battle.

The creature stared at his tool, held ready like a sword. It was polished to a shine, reflecting moonlight as easily as it would the sun.

"Steel has no effect on us, human!" the thing spat, then lunged forward with a laugh.

Erwan swung his scythe in a wide arc, shifting his body as if reaping corn from a tall stalk. The creature was quick and tried to block, but the farmer had made this movement countless times in his life. To the ground rolled a wicked head, red eyes and sharp fangs smiling upward at the night sky, harvested cleanly at the base of its neck.

The others skidded to a halt.

Erwan now recognized these creatures as voltur. His grandfather had spoken of them, told tales of spindly specters with inhuman strength and speed. Each voltur had once been human before death. Now, if the myths were to be believed, they roamed the night as revenants, reanimated to quench an insatiable thirst for human blood.

But they had not been reanimated by chance, to become a voltur meant to have been killed and drained by a vampure.

"Iron," one of them shrieked, and both backed away.

"I do not fear him," the second growled despite recoiling. It sniffed the air. "He is only human."

"He has seen us," the first argued, its eyes locked on the blood dripping from the scythe, "and must not be allowed to interfere with Goro's plans!"

Erwan's ire was too much not to hold back. His mind remembered the bloody teeth of Dominus Titus, the casual wipe of his lips as if he had devoured a greasy meal, and fitfully raged.

His family must *not* rise as these monstrous forms.

His scythe moved like an extension of the farmer's arm, hacking and slicing skin and sinew from cowering creatures. Moving again as if harvesting his field, Erwan gleaned bone and muscle, ripping them asunder and hacking their undead forms into pieces.

Rage filled him, a torrent of strength fueled by anger, until nothing remained to dismember.

Panting and out of breath, Erwan raced into his hovel.

The sight waiting for the husband and father, now drenched in his enemy's blood, brought him at once to his knees. Rupert and Racinda lay still on the dirt floor. He scanned their bodies for injury, finding only the tiniest of puncture marks on the base of each neck. From there they had been drained, robbed of youthful innocence and any chance they once had for the happiness their father once found.

You must kill them with a dragon's tooth, a distant memory whispered, his grandfather's voice preparing a terrified child for this moment. *Or sever their heads from their torsos with an iron blade.*

Erwan held that iron in his hand, clutching and squeezing its blood-swelled, wooden handle. He raised that hand, prepared to do what must be done, but found he could not. These were his children, his beloved and most favored of all accomplishments. They were the best of him. How could he send them to the afterlife, even should they emerge as undead?

Staring at the bodies, sadness consumed the father. Inside, regret and anger dueled for control of his mind. He had to do the act. He had to remove their precious heads from their shoulders like his grandfather had taught. They were no longer human, neither Rupert nor Racinda any longer, but voltur who would devour their own father should they awaken—and they would, as revenants and shadows of their former selves.

Erwan wept uncontrollably. *What if they could have been saved?* he wondered. Then another thought struck him, forcing movement into his legs and ripping his eyes from the unfatherly act he almost committed. *Adelia!*

Where was his wife?

He rushed across the hovel, sprinting to the closed door leading to the bedroom. What unfathomable horror waited just beyond? What would he find of his wife and, if still alive, would she curse him forever for the deed he had considered?

A crimson hand, stained by the sin of failure as a protector, slowly lifted the latch and pushed open the portal. Erwan closed his eyes, breathed a deep breath, then let it out. He was ready to die and would give himself over to whatever waited on the other side. Stepping through, he looked upon the bed upon which he had first lain with his beautiful bride.

That bridal passion had been repeated, but not by him nor enjoyed by Adelia.

Quilts and furs lay discarded on the ground, unable to warm his wife's lifeless form forever now like ice. She too had been drained of lifeforce.

Erwan, having failed as a husband as well as a father, raised his scythe but again refused to bring it down. Despite the warnings of his grandfather ringing mercilessly in his ears, he had lost every-thing, and would not allow himself to reap the last remnants of humanity. There had to be another way to prevent evil from rising in his family's form.

For the better part of evening, Erwan's life returned to dirt. With a shovel he dug and with a hoe he cleared rocks, digging deep enough to keep wild scavengers away from his loved ones. Into three graves he committed their remains. Into these holes he left beloved pieces of his past, wooden toys for the children and simple jewelry belonging to Adelia. He placed her most prized possession, an iron and bronze necklace around her neck, then returned to the surface to bury his own heart beneath the dirt of his legacy.

Erwan did not wash. He had no time to wade the river and might have encountered more voltur had he tried. A bath would mean setting aside his scythe, and that he would keep forever by his side for the rest of his days. Covered in bloody filth, the farmer returned to his hovel.

Though his own possessions were few, he spent precious minutes searching for a certain chest. He found it shoved deep inside another, once belonging to his father and his before him, buried beneath clean furs and a woolen blanket. The box he drew out had no splendor, a simple pine rectangle carefully hewn by hand and constructed with iron nails.

With trembling hands, Erwan lifted the lid, setting it aside.

His father's items were on top. These he knew well, two wedding bands carved from wood by the same hands that made the chest. One also belonged to Erwan's mother. He set these aside. Next came a pouch with trinkets and odds and ends inside. These were also his father's but held no value beyond sentimentality. He set these aside and drew out a single piece of fur.

This bit of leather was wrapped around a hard, flat object within. This, and everything left inside the box, were Grandfather's. Carefully peeling back the fur, he drew out a torc, a thick necklace that fit more like a collar than jewelry. Erwan examined the segments, hard scales dug up by centuries of farmers and passed down to the maker of the choker.

"I wore this when we fought against the Roman invaders," Grandfather had once told Erwan as a boy. "It will protect the wearer from any swing of a blade and from more frightening foes, as well." Having now seen voltur for himself, the farmer finally understood the meaning. This torc was made of dragon scale and would protect his neck from their bites.

Erwan put it on.

The next object inside the box was a garment, but not of the usual type for a serf. Trembling hands touched the iron links, lifting out a chain metal shirt. Erwan pulled it over his head, carefully tucking the collar beneath the torc.

Ready to leave, he packed a bit of food and a waterskin, enough to carry him to Mount Sapientia. He would need no more than that if the legends were folly. He retrieved his scythe before leaving his hovel. The place held nothing for him, not after his family had perished. Before he did, Erwan pulled a burning branch from a dying fire. With tears steaming dry from its heat, he torched everything in his home that would burn.

Erwan the Bold set off to find dragons.

A bloodstained satchel hung by his side, and inside was a gift for those he would find. Not everyone knows where to find these beasts of legend, they themselves preferring roosts far away from humans and impossible to find. They do leave clues, however, to aid the worthy in their search. Erwan knew of these from his grandfather.

"Mount Sapientia," the old man often rambled, "is home to dragons, but only the determined will find a way to climb its steep cliffs, and only the bold will be greeted atop its summit."

Erwan had always dismissed those ramblings as myth but also ignored the old man's stories about voltur and vampure. Those had leaped directly from legend into reality and, if this bold, young man were to take on Dominus Titus, he would require the aid of dragons. Thus he travelled to Mount Sapientia, protected by a shirt of chainmail, a wide torc of dragon scales, and armed with an iron scythe.

The mountain was reachable by foot, only a few hours south of Cardac. He would follow the river until it branched east, then would continue toward a high mountain ridge under the cover of forest. These lands were off limits to his people, considered sacred and full of ancient evils, but Erwan had always dismissed these claims as superstition. Now, given his newfound knowledge of such realities, he walked with scythe in hand, gripped firmly and at the ready.

With great caution, Erwan passed through the night without incident. As the forest thinned, moonlight showed him a bald mountain edged by sheer rock faces. They seemed to wrap this particular summit, denying approach from all directions. He recognized it at once as Sapientia, an ancient volcano many millennia quiet.

From far away the mountaintop appeared ripped away, its dark conical structure rising high above the rest of the mountains, too high to climb. From as close as he stood on this moonlit night, it was worse than unclimbable. To try would be certain death. Erwan did not even have a rope with which to try.

"There is a path," his grandfather once promised, "up one face of the mountain which only reveals itself to the boldest or brave. Such adventurers must be resolute in their mission, intent on making the climb, or they will miss the brief moment in which that path is revealed. If you ever attempt this journey, do not do so in darkness or full light."

At the time, though the thought of dragons mystified the child, Erwan had no intention of ever attempting the climb at all. He was born with a considerable weakness, a terrible fear of heights. As he grew to manhood there was no task he could not perform on his own unless it meant leaving the ground.

Only the summer before, his fear of heights forced him to hire another man to repair the thatch on his roof, earning laughter and ridicule and many villagers. Though the home was not tall, only a few dozen hands from its base, such a height would fill him with dizziness and cause his breath to cease. No, Erwan was most certainly a man of the dirt in all regard, and his feet were meant to remain fixed upon the earth.

That he sat basking in the moonlight, staring up at such a sheer rock face with determination to climb, spoke of his hatred and lust for vengeance against Dominus Titus. The farmer stared like this for most of the night, studying the stone and looking for handholds, calculating how many hours it would take to make the climb barring any incident. He concluded the trek would take an entire day if not more.

He decided to begin at first light.

It was not much longer before sunlight made its appearance, rising above his right shoulder and peeking out over the forest behind him. The mountain itself hid in the shadows, not quite ready to awaken. Erwan rose from his spot and stretched, finally feeling fatigue of his own. His shoulders and hips ached from sitting so long, a day of planting and a night of digging had worked its way into sedentary muscles.

He knew he should have slept, but Grandfather's words and the threat of voltur had kept him alert.

Now it was time to face his fear, to scale the rocks and climb higher than he had ever dared. One misstep or slip would mean certain death, a welcome consequence that would reunite him with Adelia and the children.

I will kill Dominus Titus, he thought, those words propelling him forward. *I will face these ancient dragons and demand they join me in battle against the Roman.* He stepped forward just as the sun peeked out fully over the treetops.

His eyes then played a trick in the morning light, pausing his feet midstride. He strained them, once more tracing the rock face. Dawn danced upon the steep surface, leading his focus along a newly revealed zigzag of shadow. The trail led all the way to the summit.

It cannot be! he thought, seeing his grandfather's promised path. He had to see more, needed to climb higher to confirm what he was seeing was true.

Without delay he rushed forward, found a handhold, and pulled his body upward until he reached another. In a matter of moments, he found himself resting on a ledge once invisible from the ground. It wasn't too wide, just large enough for a large man to walk without trouble.

Then Erwan made the mistake of looking down.

Though only three dozen hands above the ground, he teetered with vertigo, his mind swimming while heart thumped panic.

Kill Dominus Titus, he told himself, as if that mantra would keep him from falling.

It worked. His mind settled and dizziness abated. From then on he kept his eyes glued to the path three to five paces ahead of his feet.

He climbed that ridge, higher and higher, along the zigzagging path to the top. Though ancient, it held up well. Only once did he stop to rest on a larger platform that seemed intentionally carved out for this purpose. It was a cavern of sorts, but not too deep—only large enough for one human to rest their limbs far enough away from the edge. He could have napped here, if desired, and almost did.

But a nap would rob him of most of the sunlight he needed to reach the top. He kept his body alert by focusing his mind on the cavern itself. It was not natural but was not carved by human tools. Large scratch marks grooved the rock, each scrape the width of his hand, as if sharp claws scraped away the softer formations and left only the granite.

He leaned out and looked across, eyeing the next ledge beside where he rested. Before sleep could overwhelm him, Erwan continued his trek, noticing something strange the higher he ascended. The height no longer bothered him as much as it had. Several times he found he could look out over the valley below, marveling at how small the distant village now seemed. In fact, his entire life seemed inconsequential. All that occurred before Dominus Titus ripped his family away meant nothing.

I'm bound for something bigger, he told himself, running his hand along the rock wall and feeling the traces of dragon mark. *I never mattered to the world but now will make a mark of my own.* His mind swam with thoughts of revenge, of impaling and slicing apart the Roman overseer. Anger pushed him upward, higher toward the clouds now obscuring the summit.

He almost didn't notice the ledge when it crumbled away beneath his weight.

It was only a small section that gave out but proved enough to send him plummeting downward. Desperate fingers dug at the pathway before him as he slid, his feet and waist dangling over the side where rock had crumbled from weather and age. Tiny trails of blood smeared the ledge as he clung, scrapping and clawing for a grip. Abruptly he caught one with both hands, just as his chest swung downward.

The lower path loomed far below the farmer's feet, dangling and kicking as his hands throbbed and ached above. If he let go he would surely have died. There was no room to catch his balance if he did not bounce completely off instead.

Erwan had to force himself to breathe, to remain calm despite his pending doom. If only his arms did not ache so badly, muscles worn out from planting, swinging his scythe, and digging those graves. Maybe it would have been easier to pull himself upward, to climb onto the path and leave the broken section behind him had he not wasted the energy on his family.

I'm so tired, he complained in his mind. *If I let go, I can join them in death, can end this charade of false heroics!*

The need for revenge once again surged to the forefront, giving strength enough to pull himself upward and forward with bleeding fingertips. With only hatred of the Roman to fuel him, he crawled onto the ledge, rose to his feet, and continued as if death had not tried to rob him of that vengeance.

Dominus Titus must die, he said again, over and over as if speaking the act into existence. Soon, he spoke it aloud, "Dominus Titus, of Rome, must die."

Thus, Erwan reached the summit of Mount Sapientia.

As he topped the highest ridge, he found himself gradually descending into an ancient depression. Long ago, perhaps millions of years, the top of Sapientia had ripped away in an explosion of rocky debris that littered the valley beneath its haunches. Now, all that remained for the farmer to explore was a bowl shaped paradise.

This forest he found, warmed by the pulsing heart of the mountain, grew lush flora unlike any Erwan or any villager in Cardac had ever imagined. The broad leaves of vines and ferns thrived beneath the tall, deciduous canopy, and colorful birds and insects flittered here and there before the wide eyes of the unlikely explorer.

A roar shook the valley, a tremendous voice that trumpeted disagreement or alarm with equal annoyance. Erwan hoped within his heart the sound came from a dragon. Any other beast would bring disappointment, perhaps even enough to sway him from his quest for vengeance.

If he did not find a dragon, Erwan resolved himself to die. He glanced over his shoulder. That ledge would make the perfect jumping off point. *I will jump,* he promised himself. *If they do not exist or will not help me. I will dive over the side and cast my need for revenge against the ground.*

Another roar answered the first, one that seemed to argue feebly against the previous command. Certainly this sound came from dragons.

Erwan emerged into a clearing, an area where trees and plants refused to grow. The heat here was noticeably warmer, radiating upward from large rocks. There was also a pool, its warm water home to tiny fish darting after even smaller meals. He looked around. Here is where he expected to find dragons.

"Here me!" the farmer cried, drawing out his scythe and holding it aloft. The metal flashed sunlight except where blood still stained the iron. "I call upon dragons to aid my cause. Evil has visited mankind in the form of bloodsucking legions and posing as Roman overseers."

The farmer, having said his practiced words, paused and waited for a response. None came forth. Neither did any dragons.

Erwan had planned for this. A trembling hand reached into his second satchel, the one borne from his farm with great care. As quickly as it went in, that hand came out again with a grisly object held by the hair. He lifted the voltur head high, letting the foulness of its stench catch full on the air, then placed it on the ground and stepped back.

"Here is proof mankind needs your aid," he yelled so all nearby dragons would hear. Then, using the words his grandfather had taught him so many years before, he added, "I call upon the Ancient One to hear my cause and judge my need for aid!"

"Who are *you* to bring such vileness into our home?" a voice demanded from behind.

Erwan turned but could not find the source of the words. "I am Erwan," he replied with back straight, addressing the dark shadow beyond the trees.

Movement flashed again behind him, this time from the opposite side of the clearing. The man whirled around to watch a long dragon, snakelike in its movement with long wings pressed against its sides. The creature moved with lightning speed, snatching the voltur head up in its teeth with a single movement before retreating beyond the pool.

An aerouant, Erwan realized, recognizing its long body and swishing tail. *A protector of its kind.* It took up an aggressive stance as three more creatures appeared. These were smaller, standing on hind legs like humans. Strong arms reached behind their bodies, webbed with wings ready to make flight. They stood behind the first and he seemed ready to defend. These he recognized as wyvern.

"What say you, Dregal," the voice from the trees asked the aerouant. "Is this human worthy of your aid?"

The long creature scoffed, sending a puff of smoke into the air. "Most certainly *not,*" he said with a bit of disdain. "I can smell his unworthiness from here. He has not a shred of dragon blood, and what smears his body is from the abomination."

"Perhaps another will claim him," the voice suggested, but no other aerouants appeared. To Erwan's irritation all the dragons laughed in unison, as if the voice had made a joke. The two beside Dregal then narrowed their eyes at the farmer, swirling pools of fire that seemed to condemn his very existence. "Very well," the voice decided, "be on your way, human."

Erwan had paid close attention to the exchange, wondering at the words of Dregal. *How could a human have dragon blood?*

he wondered. Standing taller and planting his feet in defiance he demanded once more, "I call upon the Ancient One, to..."

"I know, I know," the voice roared, "to hear your cause and judge your need for aid! Well, you have been judged *unworthy* and your need for aid is moot. You killed at least one of these abominations, surely you can kill more. Voltur hardly seem worthy of our time."

"My fight is against more than just *voltur*," Erwan explained. "A *vampure* killed my family, turning them into..." he broke off, choking down the words he tried to form. "Draining them dry," he finally managed. "I need the Ancient One's help," he begged. "I don't know much about dragon rituals, but my grandfather said that only the Ancient One can judge a human's worthiness. I care not for the concerns of this aerouant, nor the little ones. I plead only to the Ancient One."

Dregal scoffed a second time, this time followed by rumbling laughter. "He knows nothing at all, this human." The beast then spread his wings, beating them fiercely before rising up into the sky. As he fled southward, the other dragons followed.

"He is right," the voice cautioned Erwan. "Dragons do not fight, we are too few in number for that and rely upon the aerouants for protection. Dregal is the fiercest of all, usually hungry for a fight but has judged you unworthy."

"I demand the *Ancient One* judge me, not that worthless Dregal."

"The Ancient One *has* judged you and found you bold and daring but also pitiful and misguided. You will not earn his aid either."

"You don't understand. This vampure, he is Dominus Titus, the Roman overseer of this region. He is the embodiment of evil, the..."

"I don't care if he is Goro himself," the voice said dismissively. "Go now, human, and return to your home."

"I have no home to return to," Erwan admitted, his voice full of defeat. Abruptly he paused. "Goro... Who is Goro?"

"Never you mind Goro."

"I've heard that name," the farmer said thoughtfully. He had heard it recently. If he could only remember where.

The voice laughed. "That name is ancient, more ancient even than me. Surely you heard it in one of your silly legends."

"No," Erwan said defiantly. "I've heard it recently, from one of the voltur, in fact! 'Goro is risen,' he said."

The voice no longer answered, deep in thought or sick of Erwan's presence. Either way his silence mocked the farmer, sending him off the way he had come.

The trip had been wasted, not a single dragon would aid his quest. He stepped into the forest and made his way to the southern cliff, thinking the entire way of where he would go and what he would do. There was nothing for him now, neither in Cardac nor in Aventicum. He had no home at all. He kept walking until he had risen to the top edge of the sloping crater and looked over the side.

"Forgive me, Adelia!" he screamed over the side, his voice echoing into the valley below. *I must jump,* he realized, *and no one would care. I am worthless to Adelia, Rupert and Racinda. Pathetic and completely unworthy of life.*

Thus, Erwan the Lamentable leaped from the cliff, his tear-filled eyes locked on the dirt waiting below. He did not cry out, nor did he flail his arms against the wind rushing by. He had accepted his fate, soon to join his wife and children in death. Final thoughts were of them.

Erwan's final plummet filled him with an odd sense of calm. Worries disappeared over the side of Mount Sapientia, his body relaxed, and his mind prepared for eternity.

One would expect panic would set in as both mind and body fought against death, but not in Erwan's case. Shock from losing his family overwhelmed him, and he gave wholly over to its grip. His heart slowed as the wind raced by, and the rest of him slowly shut down. He did not even notice when strong claws gripped him midfall.

His trance broke with a jolt, his body abruptly jerked upward, restoring the beat of his heart to normal. Erwan came suddenly alert and aware as dragon wings carried him across the sky.

He blinked his eyes, taking in the view. They had never seen the world with such beauty, a splendor that only flying revealed. He saw the world in that moment as a dragon would, small and none of his concern. Behind him Mount Sapientia grew distant while up ahead Aventicum emerged from an emerald horizon.

"Where are you taking me?" he asked the dragon without taking his eyes off the city.

"We travel to the place you requested, for the reason you boldly called upon dragonkind to aid you. We will travel to the capital city and face this tyrant you wish to depose."

Erwan recognized this voice. He had heard it speak to him upon the mountain. "So, you have judged me?" he asked the Ancient One.

"Yes, I have judged you rash and stupid, full of anger and foolish vengeance. But I also judge you bold, so much so I cannot refuse your request. To challenge this Dominus Titus is one matter, but I sense in you another fate."

"What fate is that, which caused you to pluck me before joining my family in death?"

Ignoring the question, the dragon asked one of his own. "Who is Adelia to you, for whom you called out before leaping to certain death?"

"She is my wife, killed by Dominus Titus along with our children. Tell me," Erwan urged, "why did you change your mind?"

"If Goro is truly risen as you so strongly believe, a great plague will visit this world."

"Who *is* Goro?" Erwan asked, closing his eyes to better feel the wind caressing his face.

"Goro is the embodiment of an evil so ancient, so vile, it is nearly unspeakable. He is the Lord of Blood, he who created the vampure and rules over darkness. Until now, he has been asleep for thousands of years while his brood has walked among the societies of human-kind. He is the reason dragonkind hide away, keeping our distance from humans."

"But now you will challenge him?"

"I am old and tired, too weak to challenge Goro after wasting so many of my years on this earth running from his evils. I've watched his legions tear apart my kin and devour the sanguis within their blood for too long. We were once a mighty race, strong in numbers and long-lived, but those legions withered us down to almost nothing. I am ready to die, not today, but soon, but would first like to ensure the survival of my kind."

"And killing Titus will help you do that?"

"No, killing Titus will bring me knowledge of Goro's where-abouts, a mystery that has plagued my millennium. I have a plan, but it requires sacrifice."

"What must you give up?"

The dragon laughed, a rumbling roar that shook their flight. "I must give up my form. My power is great, but I am useless as an Elderkin. I seek a form much stronger than this."

"I don't understand," Erwan admitted. "What is more powerful than a dragon?"

"Numbers, human. Numbers are stronger. The legions of Goro have hunted and destroyed us because they are many. Worse, they hide among those who are more plentiful still."

Erwan's eyes grew wide with understanding. "You are more easily hunted in your dragon form, and so you need to blend in with humans."

"So, you are intelligent as well as bold," the Ancient One remarked. "Yes. I have been waiting for a worthy host to carry my form, one who would not struggle against a bond. You are ready to die, so your loss might as well be my gain."

They slowly circled, beginning their descent far enough from the city they would not be seen. A clearing beside a glassy lake seemed to be the dragon's target for landing.

Erwan considered the dragon's offer, wondering if it was too late to back out of this fate. "Will I still exist after you take this form?" he asked.

"You will remain long enough to exact your revenge upon Dominus Titus, then I will exchange my soul for yours."

"Will *I* become the dragon, then?"

"No. You will cease to exist at all."

Erwan said nothing, focused on the promise that he would rejoin Adelia and the children in death. That single thought filled him with sadness, allowing him to finally set aside vengeance for sorrow. Instead of anger he felt loss, a terrible emptiness that begged silence. The dragon had offered him that respite, and he would gladly accept. It was a fair trade, one he already committed to when leaping off the mountainside.

I'm already dead, he thought, just before the dragon dropped him into the lake.

Erwan hit the water with a terrific splash. The coldness of it broke his thoughts and changed them immediately from melancholy to anger. He kicked hard to the surface, his lungs screaming for air. As he gasped and flailed, desperate to swim to shore, he caught sight of the Ancient One and paused mid stroke.

This dragon was different than the others he had seen on Mount Sapientia.

In all his life, having heard so many legends from both his grandfather and the storyteller in Cardac, Erwan had never imagined so many different types of dragons. Those legends had only ever mentioned two, the aerouant, and those others, the smaller, bipedal types he faced on the mountain.

No, the Ancient One was of an entirely different form than he had expected.

This beast rested his large, lumbering body atop four sets of stout legs. He seemed to be the size of four Dregals, massive and strong, with smoke billowing from his nostrils. For what seemed Erwan's benefit, the beast stood to full height and fanned huge wings that blocked the sun and shaded the entire beach. Every scale on this monstrous being was dark, a pitch black that seemed to swallow the light of the setting sun. Only his eyes shone with color, flaming yellow with swirling shades of orange and red fire.

The human pulled his dripping body from the lake, forgetting his anger and staring up with awe. This ancient beast need not hide in shadows, atop the highest mountain away from dangers, nor should it cower in a forest, hiding its form from mankind. His magnificence should be adored, worshiped by those who walk on land.

Erwan knelt.

"Who are you, human?" the Ancient One demanded.

"I am Erwan."

"I do not mean how are you called, I ask who you *are*. Are you a nobleman among your people? A warrior of great renown? Are you important in your society?"

"Quite the opposite, my lord. I am a farmer, tied to the land owned by the Roman Dominus Titus."

"Ah," the beast rumbled. "I know of these Romans. So they still plague this earth with their quest for dominance..." He trailed off into thoughtful silence while Erwan waited.

"What is your name, my lord?" the human finally asked. "How should I address you?"

"My name..." the Ancient One seemed confused by the term but quickly recovered. "I am called many things. You already know me as the Ancient One."

"Why is *that,* my lord? Are you the eldest?"

"Eldest indeed," the beast replied. "I am the first to reach this form, and the last remaining of it as well."

"So, you have many forms to choose from as dragonkind?"

"More than you humans can comprehend. We are an evolving species, changing forms as our situation dictates, but this was the final, most complete, but not for long."

"Why haven't others evolved as well?" Erwan asked. It was a simple question, and he meant no harm by it, but its asking brought forth great pain and suffering within the dragon.

The Ancient One let out what could only be interpreted as a sigh. His eyes dulled, swirling dimmer with his sadness, as he explained, "This is the elder form I wear, and once my kind were many. But we evolve slowly, the process that takes eons to achieve, and most of my Elderkin have been killed or hunted by humans and vampure with great vigor. Now, they hunt our young, like the wyvern you met upon Mount Sapientia."

"That is what they were?" Erwan asked with awe. "Those who walked on two legs? They are called wyvern?"

"Yes, and Dregal you recognized as an aerouant."

"What is the difference between the species," Erwan begged.

"Not species!" the Ancient One growled with irritation. "All dragonkind are the same, only our *forms* are different. Our young choose their next form when they enter the chrysalis. They first emerge as either aerouant or wyvern depending on their own spiritual calling. They emerge from that chrysalis reborn and reshaped until ready to enter their next. The process repeats until reaching final form."

Erwan listened carefully, barely able to contain his excitement at learning so many dragon secrets in one sitting. A thought brought a frown. "Both aerouant and wyvern are also hunted nearly to extinction, aren't they?" he asked. "That's why Dregal would not bond with me."

"Yes and no. Dregal refused the vinculum because he had already bonded one and does not desire another. After that human died, his choice was to protect our young. Bonding another human would serve his new mission no purpose."

"Why did *you* choose me?" Erwan asked timidly.

"As I explained before, my final task must be to destroy Goro. That is what has kept me alive past my desire to remain on this earth. I wish to kill him, then propagate again before transcending to the spiritual plane. You and I share a desire both for vengeance, and equally welcome death to end our pain. *That* is why I chose you, Erwan the Bold, to be my vinculum."

"But you are not an aerouant. How can you bond a vinculum?"

"I was one in my previous form, before I became of the Elderkin. I still have the power and will share it with you after I have fulfilled my promise and aided your cause."

Erwan yawned. He wanted to continue, to share this conversation deep into the night, but he desperately needed sleep. "I've been awake a full day and night," he told the Ancient One. "I must rest before we challenge Dominus Titus."

"Do so, human, while I scout the kingdom for his whereabouts."

"He should be arriving to Aventicum soon," Erwan assumed. "He travels by carriage, a red and golden one, and left Cardac less than two days ago."

The dragon nodded his massive head, then spread his wings wide. "Stay in the forest," he advised the human, "and I will find you before nightfall."

"Wait," Erwan urged. "How should I call you, Ancient One? What is the name of the one I will bond?"

"In your language my name is pronounced *Argant*." With that, Argant the Ancient rose into the air and left the human to rest.

Erwan awoke just before nightfall, the subtle change in forest sounds breaking his sleep. Thankfully, he had not dreamed, no doubt those would have been filled with terrors or memories to speed grief upon waking. He did, however, rouse with a renewed desire for vengeance.

"Dominus Titus must die," he whispered aloud before standing and stretching. His body ached from overuse, but at least his mind had regained clarity.

Finding food was no problem, there was much to forage though he wished for meat instead. He also gathered firewood, building a sizable campfire for warmth. Soon his stomach ached less than it had. He stared into the flame, tightly gripping his scythe and thinking how he would use it to strike down the Roman.

That man was no voltur. He was a centurion, a skilled fighter with a host of soldiers protecting him. How could a simple farmer emerge victorious, armed only with the tools of the field?

A rustling of branches lightly announced the arrival of a living thing. Erwan stood, brandishing his scythe at the forest.

"Put that away," Argant's voice rumbled, muffled by something between his teeth. As he emerged, he spat out a doe, its neck broken clean without a trace of blood anywhere on its dun-colored fur. "It is only me, back with a meal for us to share."

The human went to work quickly, eager for the meat his companion had provided, skinning and quartering the animal.

"Do not waste the innards nor the flesh," Argant admonished. "Take what you will need and leave me the rest of it as provided."

"You will eat it raw?" Erwan asked.

"I will eat it as it tastes the best," the dragon replied, settling down beside the fire, its warmth radiating against his snout.

Preparing the meal took no time at all. The man selected the tenderloin, placing it on a makeshift spit over the fire. The dragon consumed the rest. Argant proved a noisy eater with his crunching of bones and slurping of flesh, but thankfully was not a messy one.

Once both their bellies were full, Erwan broke the silence. "What did you find? Did Titus make it to Aventicum?"

"His carriage arrived when the sun was highest."

"Curses," Erwan cast the last few bites of his meat into the fire. He's too protected in the city, especially in the palace! How will we get to him now? I might get through the gates, but won't make it near the palace. Their archers and ballistae will attack *you* the moment you appear in the sky."

"Are you finished voicing your human negativity?" Argant asked with more than a bit of arrogance.

Erwan began to protest but was cut off in an instant.

"Silence!" the Ancient One commanded. "We dragons have powers of which your kind cannot even fathom. Since you are finished eating, we will move on. Ready your arm for swinging iron, because that will be your only task in the reaping to come." The beast stood and shook dirt and leaves from his scales, then led the human toward the lake. Frowning up at the sky, he spoke again. "Tonight will prove difficult but not impossible. Your revenge will come swiftly, but then you will aid me in my own mission. There is a temple near the palace, connected by tunnels by which the Roman will soon travel. I sensed a darkness in those catacombs, an evil that *must* be of Goro!"

"How do you know?" Erwan pressed, irritated by the shroud of mystery. Either Argant did not trust him with the knowledge or felt it beneath his understanding. Abruptly the dragon whirled, streams of fire pouring forth from his nostrils. The human backed up, teetering backward as he crashed onto the ground full of fright.

The world around him shimmered and changed. He suddenly found himself flying in the sky instead of laying in the dirt, his eyes scanning the countryside below. An object moved below, a speck at first, moving along an ant path. As his eyes dialed in, Erwan realized the path was a road, and the speck was a gilded red carriage pulled by a pair of white horses. He recognized it at once as belonging to Dominus Titus.

He repositioned in the air, moving higher so as not to be seen.

Below, the vehicle made its way to the human city of Aventicum. There was no wall around the Roman stronghold, but a wooden fortress stood nearby. These would hold both archers and ballistae. There was also a small palace, more of a domus than what would be found in Rome, and its gates opened up immediately for the carriage.

Erwan made two more high circles, his keen eyesight seeing the ground as closely as if he stood upon it. He took notice of a temple and amphitheater not far from the palace. His eyesight shifted once more, blinking new vision that seemed to sense heat instead of taking in light. What he saw with this new perspective could only be tunnels beneath the ground, as Dominus Titus and his soldiers entered the palace then somehow crossed underground beneath the streets to the temple.

The dragon abruptly took back his vision, ripping it away from the human and leaving Erwan to writhe on the ground. Seeing again with his own eyes, the farmer vomited his dinner. It took several minutes for the vertigo to subside. Argant waited patiently without a word.

"How did you do that?" Erwan finally asked. "How did you show that to me?"

"Dragonkind have different abilities than humans. Foremost, we can bend the senses of other species. Thus, I was able to show you the evidence you needed."

"All of that, what I just witnessed as if I were there, it was what you saw earlier today?"

"Yes, as *I* saw it."

"The city saw him return to the palace, but Dominus went straight into the temple using the underground tunnels?"

"Yes, but he has fed well during his outing and will need sleep. Vampure do not rest the same way as humans and will be vulnerable while his body metabolizes the sanguis he consumed." Argant knelt low to the ground, spreading his wings flat against his body. "Now, climb atop my back and be welcomed as a one-time rider of dragons."

Erwan could not believe his eyes and ears. That this mighty and ancient beast offered itself freely, humbling its body so a human could climb atop and ride it like a beast of burden, was something of which he felt undeserving. Who was he, but a farmer, a broken man without loved ones, uneducated and poorly born, to ride in such a prominent position? He bowed reverently and grabbed ahold of Argant's scales, pulling himself upward.

"You will find two spines protruding from my shoulder blades," the dragon advised. "Hold on tightly to those." With a mighty push off the ground, he beat his wings and shot upward, much faster than Erwan believed possible for such a lumbering beast.

The human felt the rush of wind as they flew upward into the night sky. Like before, when he stepped off the edge to end his life, he found himself at ease soaring towering heights. He no longer felt fear. Looking down he saw the fires of Aventicum. Each would be manned by a sentry.

I am going to die tonight, Erwan said in his mind.

"You will die," agreed the Dragon, "but so too shall Dominus Titus."

Briefly, a flicker of mourning rushed forward, grief so powerful it leaked out as a tiny sob. He choked it down quickly, hoping to hide his weakness from Argant. He held his breath as two tiny faces, pale from death stared up at him with bloodshot eyes and thirsty grins. The image changed and he saw Adelia, ravaged and drained before his eyes.

Erwan swallowed down what almost flowed as tears and asked, "How will we get past the city defenses? They will be watching the gates."

"They will also be watching the sky," Argant corrected. "The driver saw me from his carriage and Titus will be expecting me."

"You, but not me…" the dragon rider noted.

"Turn your eyes skyward and behold the power of my magic, human. See what the Romans will be watching instead of us."

All at once the stars began falling from the sky, zipping from east to west above the city, exploding upon the western horizon.

Erwan gasped to see such splendor, equally terrified as awed. "But it isn't real?" he asked. It seemed so horribly so.

"It is not real, and neither are they."

The human's eyes searched the sky, mesmerized by the streaks of light. "They, who?" he asked, blinking and refocusing. Far off to the west, illuminated by the brilliant flashes of distant explosions, flew a formation of dragons. Between strobes he counted forty in all, a mixture of Elderkin and aerouants.

Down below, in the city, more fires lit up the ground. Bells tolled and horns sounded as soldiers sprinted with torches toward the western wall. All eyes were locked on that horizon, staring down the incoming horde.

"Hold on tight," Argant warned, dipping fast and low in a dive toward the surface.

Erwan gripped as tightly as he could, digging his face into hard scales. They felt oddly warm against the biting wind, as if flame raged within the dragon's heart.

At the last moment, just before Erwan thought they would crash to their deaths, a mighty beating of wings sent dirt and rock flying into the night. Argant sailed low, beneath the sight of the sentries and cloaked by the darkness of shadow. While they watched the west, the dragon and his rider approached swiftly from the east.

The wooden palisade loomed ahead, encircling the city. A lone sentry stood upon it, staring westward at the illusion lighting up the sky. Erwan watched with horror as Argant opened wide his jaws, catching and tossing the soldier back into his gullet. The dragon swallowed its meal midair, gliding over rooftops without deviating from course.

An amphitheater opened up beneath the beast and its rider, a Roman built coliseum for chariot races and gladiator events. The pair glided to a landing in its center, sending a cloud of dirt in every direction. Erwan looked around worriedly. *Have we been seen?* he wondered. With all attention to the western sky, he hoped they had not.

A shout from the far side of the arena proved him wrong.

The man who spied their landing was no mere sentry. The legionary had already drawn his sword, faced with a decision to flee and sound the alarm, or to rush the new arrivals and attempt to slay the dragon on his own. His hesitation suggested the choice was difficult.

As soon as he reached the dragon, Argant disappeared from sight, reappearing behind the man. The dragon let out a roar, loud enough only to turn the man's attention but not to attract other soldiers nearby. The legionary spun and lunged at the scaly beast, plunging his sword into nothingness. As soon as the tip of his blade pierced the illusion, it puffed away into a cloud of mist. At the same time the hulking black dragon reappeared, standing where it had been before. As the man turned, giant teeth snapped down upon him, slicing the leather cuirass in two. With one more bite, this soldier also became a meal.

"I will have such indigestion tomorrow," the dragon complained, lumbering past a stunned Erwan as he belched smoke and sulphury flame. He led the human to a steel gate opening into a tunnel beneath the main structure. Argant heaved his entire weight against the barrier, ripping it from its hinges and leaving it to swing unsteadily. "Come," he commanded and Erwan obeyed. "This tunnel connects to others, and one of those will take us beneath the palace. The nobility use these passages to avoid walking among the commoners."

Erwan watched as the dragon squeezed his body into the opening, crawling low. Below ground the man felt less confident than before. There was barely room to swing his scythe should the need arise, much less for a dragon to turn and help if trouble attacked from behind.

For several hundred paces, the farmer could scarcely do more than breathe deeply and try to slow his pounding heart. *What if they can hear it?* he wondered, thinking of the vampure and voltur.

But Argant seemed unfazed by both the darkness and the potential dangers ahead, boldly crawling forward and lighting the way with puffs of flame that sizzled more than roared. After several minutes they emerged in a larger chamber.

"We are beneath the palace," the dragon suggested.

Erwan cautiously eyed a side tunnel, afraid patrolling guards would suddenly step out of its shadows to give challenge. The metal grate blocking the opening remained firmly locked in place, virtually impossible to breech from the inside. Its well-oiled hinges showed frequent use, a sure sign Argant had assumed correctly and the Roman overseer waited ahead.

"He will be sleeping when we find him," the Ancient One explained, "but his legion will not. They are tasked with guarding his slumber so expect a tremendous fight," he warned. "Come, the temple lies ahead."

"How do you know he'll be sleeping? What happens if he isn't?"

"He *will* be. A vampure cannot consume as much sanguis as Titus has, not without hibernating after. His body needs time to digest it all."

Erwan gripped his scythe, eyes locked on the dragon's back. The passage here was larger, allowing the beast to walk upright with room to turn on either side. The farmer should have felt more courageous, but expectation of battle was always worse than the heat of it. The day before, when he had killed the voltur, was now a thrill he craved over this anxious waiting. The unknowing of what lie ahead consumed him, racing his thoughts and nearly sending his heart into panic.

What if I can't kill again? he wondered.

He did not have to wait long to find out. A patrol of legionaries appeared as a tight group of bobbing torches. In the flickering light, Erwan counted four men draped in crimson robes. Gilded embroidery lined the hoods covering hidden faces, glistening against the torchlight and casting a glow of its own. Thankfully, the light muted the distance these Romans could see, so they were nearly upon Argant before he opened his eyes, revealing two fiery orbs. The men froze in terror at the sudden appearance, their hands too slow when drawing weapons.

The inner warrior inside the farmer awakened, his arm moving as if it belonged to someone else. He attacked the nearest sentry, stepping forward and slicing upward into a soft armpit. With that artery severed, a crimson geyser erupted. He wrenched downward, pulling free his weapon and reaped again, this time into an inner thigh. With a pivot he moved behind the squad and paused before striking another.

Something was wrong, he smelled it more than sensed it. The scores he had just cut now steamed where they once bled, the result of iron making contact with vampure skin. The vapor burned Erwan's nostrils with the sickening smell of rancid meat.

That sentry, who should have fallen to the ground by now, turned angrily to face Erwan while his comrades squared off against the dragon. As he feared this was no man, staring up with bloody orbs lacking the whites of human eyes. These swirled hypnotically, angrily searching for the farmer who only paused for less than a heartbeat. That brief hesitation nearly cost Erwan's life as the legionary attacked with blinding speed and surging thirst.

Erwan moved as fast as he could to fight off the creature, backing as the scythe swung wildly, avoiding sharp claws that should have been hands. These sliced his skin, reaching for the weapon. Protruding from bloody lips, two fangs bit for the human's neck.

Beyond this vampure Argant engaged the other three, biting and clawing with a fury of his own. Like a dueling pack of wolves, the soldiers attacked the dragon who seemed to watch as if seeing them move in slow motion. Each bite was met with an attack or parry of his own and they never gained advantage.

Finally, Erwan managed an offensive move, one that paid off with another contact of sharp iron upon skin. The Roman was accustomed to fighting trained warriors, not farmers skilled at reaping wheat and rye. When Erwan moved, he threshed, sweeping low across the ground while the vampure moved high to bite his neck. As the iron scraped across two ankles it severed both calf muscles, sending the creature snapping forward off balance. It crashed hard on its face, both fangs bared and biting hard into solid stone. They, and the surrounding teeth, shattered upon impact.

Erwan finished his reap with a solid swing to the creature's neck, sending sparks as the tool scraped rock. Then he turned to watch Argant. With two soldiers lying dead on the floor, the dragon finished off his final adversary with a chomp and a fiery burp. After the fighting had ended, the severed remains of three vampure glowed brightly in his surging flame.

"Well done," the dragon told the farmer, pointing a bloody claw further down the tunnel. "You go on, continue down that corridor alone for two furlongs but be careful. This is the last of the patrols, but there will be guards around Dominus Titus."

"You want me to take them on by myself? I barely handled *one*!"

"Yes. I cannot sneak or move stealthily like a man, and so you must do the next part alone. I will be there when you need me, but not a moment sooner. I assure you, the vampure will be sleeping. You will only have to fight his lesser formed kin."

"Lesser formed?" Erwan demanded, pointing to the burning bodies. "Is *that* what these are, a lesser form of vampure?"

"Yes. Like dragonkind, the vampure take on many forms during their evolutionary process. They were once great beasts, but each form takes them closer to the appearance of man. Many of whom you encounter will be recently turned by Titus himself, and he will not allow his subjects to achieve a higher form without his blessing. Their hierarchy is unique to them, with one lord dividing power among many vassals. Those most trusted are bequeathed a new form when given a new region to rule over in their lord's name. The process ensures allegiance and demands fealty if not loyalty."

"I understand," Erwan lied. He knew little even about the Roman lords, and this new system confused him even more. He changed the subject. "I have only seen a few of your forms," Erwan asked, "and the Elderkin is *far* from human, but the wyvern is closer. Why do they seek human form while you seek the opposite?"

"We once believed the form of Elderkin was the highest we could obtain on this earth. We ruled this land, looking down our snouts at mammals and seeing a lesser species. We were wrong. Our dwindling numbers are proof of that. We should have embraced the resilience of man and respected their intelligence. Instead of making *them* serve *us*, we should have led mankind toward greatness. Our pride may result in the final destruction of dragonkind."

"And the vampure? How are they growing in numbers instead of dwindling? Why haven't we noticed them among us?"

"They walk among their prey as wolves hidden among sheep, eating at will, but know better than to draw attention. They have mastered humankind by whispering into ears, nudging society into whatever direction best serves their masters hidden in shadow. While humanity *believes* they are in charge, they always do the bidding of Goro, his lords, and their vassals. We should have sought out a similar form long ago, one which would allow us to disappear among humans just as they have."

"Is that what you demand of me?" Erwan asked. "After we slay Titus, will you use me to create this new form?"

"I *told* you I would! When the time comes, after your revenge is complete, I will allow you to make your sacrifice. At that time, I *will* merge our bodies into one form."

Erwan gripped the reaping scythe silently, considering. It was a fair trade, for he had nothing left worth living for. After killing Titus, he *would* choose death. The dragon could have his form. He held the blade closer while inspecting the iron. It had become a part of him over these past few days, and he hated that it represented death instead of bounty. He only needed it a bit longer.

"Time is wasting, human. Go. Find the vampure and kill him in his sarcophagus."

The farmer nodded without looking at the dragon. Bending over, he pulled a robe from the least bloodied corpse, shook it, and placed it over his head. Then he went on alone. Each step took him closer to facing the killer, the monster who consumed his family. He struggled against the urge to sprint ahead, to rush headlong into danger and end himself while avenging this nobleman's crimes.

Carefully he crept, with weapon held ready.

As he rounded the final bend, his eyes adjusted to flickering lights ahead. Fires burned beneath the temple, lighting the catacombs and casting shadows. Erwan quickly pulled the hood lower, hiding his face. The cavern was a temple of its own, hidden beneath the larger place of worship above. Crypts lined the walls and a dozen worshippers knelt in the middle, cloaked by the same gilded robes as Erwan.

Chanting echoed through the chamber, a harmonic summoning of their god. "Life Bringer," they sang, "bless us with longevity. Lord of Blood, grant us sanguis."

Atop a raised pulpit, standing over a grooved altar meant for the collection of blood, stood their devil lord.

Dominus Titus was not asleep, nor was he hidden away in a sarcophagus as Argant had promised. With arms raised behind the altar, dressed in his finery, he led the cultists in their incantations.

He had changed. Instead of a man, he loomed with outstretched wings, each leathery and bat-like. His face still resembled the Roman, and was most certainly him, but his skull was now lined with boney protrusions that stood out like horns around the crown of his head.

"May this sacrifice be pleasing," the worshippers sang in unison, "a gift from your chosen few."

The eyes of Titus scanned the room, pools of swirling blood locked in glassy orbs. "Our lord finds it pleasing," he intoned, "and blesses all his children with eternal youth." He leaned over the sacrifice, placing his arm on the altar and using it to brace his full weight. His lips curled into an exaggerated smile.

Only then did Erwan notice the sacrifice, a child tied to that altar. Her head lay between his arm and his mouth. Dressed in a flowing gown of pure white linen, the young girl never struggled. She slept as if in a drugged state, peaceful as the cultists chanted louder.

"Her life to us, our lives for you, Goro!"

Titus' teeth, pearly from his privileged position and noble breeding, transformed as they came closer to the flawless skin of the offering. Long fangs slowly extended from his gums, sharp and ready to draw nourishment from her lifeforce.

The girl's head turned toward his arm, awakened and looking through the cultists. flinching with pain as the monster touched lips to her neck It was then, during that brief moment she seemed to draw pleasure from the intrusion on her body, when Erwan recognized his daughter.

"Racinda!" he screamed.

Every hooded head turned toward the intruder. The shocked, staring faces were not human. Like Titus, their crimson eyes swirled and fangs descended from pale gums. But these worshippers, like the legionaries in the catacombs, were different than their dark lord. They were without wings or the boney protrusions Erwan now recognized as horns. They still appeared more human than voltur or vampure.

Hate filled Erwan, surging forth and entering his hand in the form of his scythe. The tool seemed to raise on its own as it swung on the nearest worshipers. Filled with rage he struck down what appeared to be a Roman man and woman by the garb worn beneath their vestments. Blindly the farmer reaped, with eyes locked on Dominus Titus, walking forward and striking down any creature who dared step in his way. He cut down six before angry thirst consumed the others. They leapt on him at once, clawing and biting at the dragon scale collar around his neck.

"Do not consume his sanguis!" Dominus Titus bellowed from the altar. "Hold him there but do *not* feast!"

Erwan felt only a dozen hands latch onto his body, but it may as well have been a hundred. The strength of these vampure gripped him so tightly he could not even struggle. One of them ripped the scythe from his hand, flinging it aside with a sizzling cry.

"Iron!" it screamed, wincing from the pain. Erwan grinned up at the beast, a Gaulish man, well-bred and properly groomed. Though not a Roman, he was certainly treated as nobility in their city.

"Move aside," Titus growled, stepping forward. He had taken the time to free little Racinda and led her toward Erwan with a held hand. "Who is this man to you?" he asked her calmly.

"He was my father," she replied dryly, without any bit of emotion in her voice.

"*Was* your father," Titus agreed. "Farmer, what is your name?"

"I am Erwan and *she* is Racinda, but... I don't understand. How are you alive, my dear? I found you and Rupert *bled out* by this beast!"

"Rupert..." Titus considered. "Ah yes. The boy. That *was* his name." Turning to the Gaul with the singed hand he ordered, "fetch the boy."

"Yes, fetch him and hand my children over to me," Erwan demanded, "and we'll be leaving."

Titus laughed, his devilish horns pointing upward while his fangs glistened downward in the torchlight. "My," he said, "aren't you a *bold* one. Erwan the Bold is what I'll call you. But no, these are not your children. Yours have died and these have been raised as mine."

The Roman released Racinda and knelt, crawling forward, then slithering like a snake atop Erwan's body, breathing close and sniffing his skin and clothing. Deft fingers unlaced the dragon scale collar, the feeling of the creature so close to his neck repulsed Erwan. With his arms and legs still held by the vampure he could only turn his head toward his daughter while bracing for the bite to come.

Her eyes had changed, now dull and dark but so unmistakably red. A bit of blood dripped from the side of her mouth. He scanned her for injuries. Other than the gaunt paleness of her skin and a pair of sunken cheeks, only her eyes appeared changed.

"My daughter," Erwan begged, "don't you want to leave with me?" He felt the foul body of the vampure press harder against his own, but Erwan only focused on his child, standing and staring at her father with strange curiosity. "Why don't you stop him?" the farmer asked his daughter. "Draw the dagger from his side and use it. Help me, daughter."

"I don't want to help you," she answered. "I'm too hungry!" She lunged, pushing past the Roman with bared fangs and biting wildly for Erwan's neck.

Titus reached out a hand, grabbing the girl and stopping her just before making contact. Her hot breath burned her father's skin, so close he could almost feel her fangs. "No. Do not taint your recent meal with *his* blood," the vampure warned.

The words made no sense. Erwan again noticed the trail of blood on her chin, realizing she must truly have feasted. His eyes then slowly focused on Titus' wrist. Two small puncture marks bled only slightly, with the same spacing as Racinda's descended fangs. He had it wrong. Titus had not drunk of his daughter. *She* had consumed *him*!

A feeling of dread wracked the farmer's insides as bile rose in his throat. He coughed and sputtered as it burned his mouth. His beloved daughter, whom he had buried on the farm, had risen as the damned.

By then the Gaulish nobleman had returned. Rupert followed, holding hands with a Roman woman and wearing the same white gown as his sister. His skin was just as pale as hers, and stretched against his skull as if he had not eaten in weeks. He licked his lips wildly as the vampure led him in, snapping and biting the air between him and his father on the ground. He too dribbled blood from the fangs protruding from his little mouth, and the wrist of the woman's robe was coated in the same.

Both of Erwan's children had risen from their grave and drank of vampure sanguis.

Dark realization filled the farmer, and he returned his gaze to Dominus Titus. "Where is Adelia?" he demanded. "Where is my wife?" She too may be nearby.

"Something isn't right," Titus said absently, ignoring the question and sniffing Erwan's neck. "Your blood is *different* than your children!" He breathed deep and added, "They only took after their mother." He sniffed once more then recoiled. Behind his fangs Titus frowned. "You are fully human and only *reek* of dragon! You've recently been around their forms!" He sniffed again. "Elderkin, most recently!"

These words confused Erwan. "My wife is also human," he stubbornly rejected the notion she could be anything else.

"She is of dragonkind, and that's why I called your children to me, to drink of my blood in this current form. They have chosen a new form, a mix between two Keryx and far nobler than any single vampure or dragon! They have *chosen* to serve Goro!"

"I don't believe you! My wife is as human as them and me! Where is she? I will ask her myself."

"Adelia is dead where you buried her. She could not be raised because of the trinkets of iron you left in her grave!" the vampure snapped. "Now answer me, Erwan the Bold, how is it I smell dragon on your body? What is this form you have taken?"

"I am not of their blood and this is no form. I am merely a vinculum."

Titus looked up hungrily, watching the tunnel from which Erwan had entered the sanctuary. "You are bonded? If so, you are the first to do so in a thousand years!"

"My lord!" the Gaulish nobleman remarked. "If he has brought his dragon here, we should feast on its sanguis and our youthful blessings will last decades!"

But Titus wavered, suddenly concerned. His blood filled eyes betrayed fear. "I smelled Elderkin. What is the name of the aerouant you have bonded?"

The farmer smiled. "His name is Argant!"

Everyone in the room gasped. Whispers of *pure blood* and *greatness* rippled through the assemblage. The Gaulish nobleman cried out, "Argant is the oldest, the first! He is the Lord of Fire! If we drink from a Keryx our blessings will endure *immortality* that rival only Goro's!"

"You fools," Titus warned without taking his eyes from the tunnel. "None of you can match Argant in your present forms! Nor do you have permission from Goro to do so!"

As if in agreement, a mighty roar echoed down the tunnel and into the sanctuary. The walls shook and torches flickered.

That was all the vampure needed. Greedy for the sanguis, the six vampure holding Erwan released him, sprinting from the sanctuary with all the others.

Still atop the farmer, Titus watched them leave, shaking his head at their foolishness. "You all rush to your deaths!" he called out, then returned his eyes to Erwan. "How are you not bonded to an aerouant instead? Why did Argant leave the safety of Mount Sapientia?" He paused, not waiting for an answer and worriedly added, "And why did he send you to face me alone?"

"He's helping me to slay *you*," Erwan spat, "and then I'll give him the means to defeat Goro!"

The Roman again eyed the tunnel through which his followers had foolishly rushed. Shouts and screams now echoed through the catacombs, mixing with an angry dragon's roar. Titus pulled his eyes away, locking them on the woman now holding the hands of

Rupert and Racinda. She seemed eager to flee and so now did Titus. He shifted his weight just slightly, taken aback by the sudden change of events.

Erwan pushed with all his strength, sending the vampure rolling to the side. As the dominus toppled, Racinda let go of the woman's hand and lunged forward. Her fangs barely missed her father's neck, just as his hand drew the Roman dagger from the dominus' belt. While his daughter's momentum carried her past, he plunged the blade forward, aiming between Titus' ribs.

The vampure let out a gasp, a silent scream as the steel struck his side, but that gasp quickly turned to laughter as the blade shattered into pieces.

Erwan stared at the useless hilt in his hand.

Titus found his balance and rose to his knees, shoving Erwan away as if he had flung a small animal. His strength rivaled ten men and the farmer skidded across the sanctuary. The dominus stood over the fallen man, flanked on both sides by Rupert and Racinda, shadows of their former selves now craving the lifeforce within their father. Their hunger was all that drove them, and two sets of bloody eyes stared lustfully, craving a meal. Both lunged.

Erwan spied the discarded scythe laying nearby, but it was out of reach.

The children reached him, clawing at his neck. It took all his strength to hold them at arm's length, snapping and biting and driven only by their need for satiation. Tears clouded the father's eyes as he stared at the discarded scythe. He would have to release one of his children to grab it, but who? The other would be upon him the moment he did.

Erwan took a gamble.

Loosening his grip on both, he rolled toward the scythe. The children clamored and fell, each pulling the other away like drowning swimmers desperate for air. While they fought, Erwan moved out of reach. His grandfather's words echoed once more.

Sever their heads, the apparition demanded.

Erwan swung the iron two times, once for each of his children, and began a journey no parent should ever endure. He no longer saw them as his own children, he didn't even see them through human eyes. He had become the scythe and the tool cared naught but for reaping. Filled with fury he gave it that pleasure, until nothing remained that resembled his children.

"You idiot!" Argant bellowed as he lumbered into the room. "They had not fully changed and could have been cured by *my* blood! That's the reason I let you go ahead, for you to sacrifice yourself so that *they* could be our future! You just squandered your last opportunity to live out your days as their father!"

Erwan, upon hearing the dragon's words, fell to his knees beside the bodies of his children.

An amused Titus stared up at the massive Elderkin, slowly reasoning out the dragon's plan. "You sent your child into the human world, hoping she would give birth in that form, producing mixed breed dragon-humans you could someday use against us? You *wanted* them to be turned vampure, so that you could intervene at the last moment when their minds had not yet accepted their new form. You hoped they would become *hybrids,* just as Goro had sought to create for so long?"

Erwan heard these words and looked up at the Elderkin. "Is this true?" he demanded.

The dragon moved clumsily, his belly swollen from so many devoured vampure. He let out a long and rumbling burp, his fire surging brightly and lighting the sanctuary, then made his way toward Titus, growling and hissing fire as the vampure backed away.

"You astound me, Erwan the Brash!" Argant said without taking his eyes from his prey. "What kind of *father* are you? You left alive the very man you sought to kill and instead hacked your own children into pieces!"

"Do *not* evade my question? Is what he said true!" the farmer screamed. "Did you let me come in here alone, hoping I would be bitten? That my own *children* would feed off me? Is *that* the evolution your kind hope to create? To become *hybrids* like Titus says?"

Argant roared again, swinging his broad tail at the ducking Roman. "You pledged me your life when we bonded, so it matters not what I do with your body *or* those of my grandchildren. You had already given up on living!" the dragon accused. "Knowledge they lived would have dampened your vengeance."

Erwan paused. It was true. Had he known they had been raised, but could have still been saved, would he still have pledged his body to this beast? He might have looked for a way out of the bond. "I deserved the truth," he argued, eyeing his scythe. Dark blood dripped from the blade to the floor. He no longer deserved to live, a failure as a husband, as a protector, and now ultimately as a father.

I know what needs to be done, he realized.

Argant snapped at Titus, his teeth ripping a gash in the vampure's wing, but the Roman moved fast, stepping aside and plunging sharp claws between hard scales. With a heave, two ripped away. The dragon roared angrily, swatting the creature away with a massive arm. He loomed over the stunned demon, his teeth biting down to rid the world of one more vampure.

With a single motion, Erwan earned his title. He boldly pressed the tip of his scythe beneath his breastbone, gripping the handle with both hands. Though he promised Argant the use of his body, he would make the deceiver earn it while also paying for his lies. "You may have my form as promised," Erwan yelled, "but Titus will also kill *you* if you take it from me now!"

"Not yet!" Argant roared.

Erwan plunged the iron deep, arching it upward into his heart, then slumped immediately to the ground. The ringing in his ears drowned out the battle across the room. Soon his vision tunneled and he could only see the dragon he had betrayed. Argant's head reared. A mixture of shock and anger filled his fiery eyes. *So, this is death,* the human thought. He had expected more pain.

The farmer died with a smile on his face, his thirst for vengeance quenched against all who had stolen away his family, Dominus Titus, Argant the Ancient, and Erwan the Bold.

Argant watched the human die, a selfish act, his taking of his own life. *Selfishness,* the Ancient One thought, *worthy of a dragon.* That had been the true downfall of his kind, their arrogance. Sadly, he had intended to allow the farmer to live until his children had formed their chrysalis and chosen their new forms, but the fool had seen only treachery when his mind failed to understand the way of dragons.

So focused on Erwan's dying smirk, Argant nearly forgot about the vampure. As the fangs bit deep into his exposed neck, he realized little time remained. If he were to take his form, blending human with dragon, the Ancient One must do it before both of them ceased to live.

The bond between vinculum and aerouant is uniquely strong, but even more powerful when bonded with Elderkin. That was the reason the advanced form usually refused humans, and why Argant had chosen this particularly bold one. What he failed to realize, was that the vinculum pair also shared grief, this man for his family and the dragon for his dwindling race. This pain amplified their union and sped the transference of sentience.

Argant should have been able to fight off Dominus Titus. He had expected to finish him off with a single bite. But consuming so many vampure had slowed him, and the sanguis acted like poison to his body. He would have to hasten the conveyance, swapping souls with his vinculum. All consciousness rushed from dragon to man, snapping blue eyes open just as they closed.

What once was Erwan blinked, and those orbs changed briefly to fire then back to blue. Argant watched his former self through these eyes, as the lumbering Elderkin fought against the vampure across the room. It collapsed atop Titus, just as the leech bit deep and began draining sanguis. From this new vantage point everything resembled a dream.

Argant rose upon two feet, for the first time since his existence. (He had never walked the earth as a wyvern.) He grabbed the wooden handle protruding from his chest. He drew it out with a grunt. The resulting pain, though expected, angered the Ancient One but also let him know the transfer had completed as he had hoped. He walked toward his former body, feeling the new one easily repair itself with Keryx sanguis.

The Lord of Fire had finally taken human form.

I am the first dragon walker, he realized, raising Erwan's scythe above his head. For a brief moment he pitied the vampure and cocked his head to watch the creature feed. *Drink heartily,* he urged him, *as much as you dare!*

Dominus Titus the Abominable had grown drunk on sanguis but had not yet realized what he drank. Titus had recently consumed pure sanguis, but would not be able to absorb what was now offered by the dragon. So young and naïve, he had expected to find only that same meal from the Elderkin's flesh, but Argant had intentionally consumed too much vampure. The Roman now consumed the poison of his own kind.

This alone would kill him.

Normally passed quickly by a dragon after eating, Argant had held the vile sanguis in, allowing it to fester and collect in the case of this very scenario. He knew that humans were unpredictable and doubted Erwan would remain true to their agreement. This final assurance would kill the vampure. Titus was a favorite of Goro, created by the Dark One himself, and his demise would serve as a lure.

Without swinging the scythe, Argant fulfilled Erwan's final task of vengeance. He had killed Titus the Abominable. The deaths of Rupert and Racinda saddened him, had slowed his plans to defeat Goro, but other opportunities would emerge in time. All the Ancient

One must do is wait and watch, spreading his seed until opportunity once again presented itself.

"Run," Argant told the Roman woman looking on, "back to Goro and tell him what has happened here today. Tell him the war is resumed, and that I *will* find him."

Part II

Chapter Fifteen

Kado stretched and yawned, finding a large object curled up beside him. He touched it, feeling hard scales and how they seemed strangely warmer than the dying fire. It rhythmically moved up and down while breathing beneath his hand. The boy opened his eyes to find two large pools of swirling fire looking up, almost smiling as he awoke.

"Good morning," the aerouant said with a bit of a rumble. Her hot breath was not offensive, and Kado actually found it soothing in the chilly cave.

"Good morning," he said with a shy smile. She had not startled him, but his eyes widened with surprise, amazed to find the aerouant had grown so large in a single night. Once the size of a lizard, she was now slightly taller than a calf, with a curling tail that wrapped around her vinculum with care. "We haven't actually officially introduced," the boy offered. "I'm called Kado."

"I know you already, Kado. I chose you, remember?"

"Yes, I understand that now." Thinking of his dreams, he asked her, "In my sleep I dreamed of the other aerouant I met, the one named Dregal. I shared his mind as we flew over a battlefield, and he thought of you."

The aerouant snorted softly, sending sparking embers to reignite the fire. "He does not think much of me, that one." She seemed irritated by his lack of acceptance, but her eyes continued to smile.

"He knows you are on your own path and understands that you chose me, and not the other way around." Kado offered. He paused, swallowing some pride before adding, "I'm sorry I kicked at you before. I saw you as a tiny thing not worth much help at all, but

I was wrong. I'm..." He paused, choosing his next words carefully. "I'm grateful you are with me. I don't understand this bond, yet, but I think I'm beginning to."

The swirling embers blinked and Kado was now certain he detected a smile on the face of the aerouant.

"We are now inseparable, you and I," she explained. "I am sworn as your protector."

"Why me? And how have you grown so much in a single night after being so small before? How do you speak so much better?" he asked. He had so many questions now that she could talk fluently.

"As *you* grow, I grow," she explained.

Kado glanced at the voltur bodies in the corner, now sunken and desiccated, mummified even, and wondered. "By killing *those*, we grew?"

A soft rumbling resembling laughter shook them both. "No, child. By conquering fear, we both grew. You grew more than me, but my change is more visible."

"I see..." But he did not yet, at least not fully. "I also dreamt of my father," he said, changing the subject. "Was that real? Did he survive the battle?"

The aerouant wrapped a wing around the boy, holding him close when she said, "The Ancient One commanded you to dream truth, and you did. As for the outcome, we have no way of knowing for sure. Part of courage is to never lose sight of hope, even when all seems lost. At least now you know the war has ended and the survivors will soon return to their homes.

"We have to find the voltur legion, don't we?" Kado asked, with fear shaking his voice.

"We do. The Ancient One spoke true. You climbed Mount Sapientia to save your village, and by doing so doomed it to the wrath of the voltur. The vampure who leads them will not be happy when he learns we murdered two members of his legion in their sleep. He will seek vengeance of his own. To complete your quest, you must face the consequences of your courageous acts."

"Since I killed some, I must kill them all?"

"Yes," she answered sadly. "For now killing is the only path you tread."

"I don't want to be a killer," the boy admitted. "At first I wanted to, I wanted to kill Lars, but now..." He paused, unsure of what he truly wanted.

"But now?" the aerouant gently encouraged him to go on.

"Now, I only want my family all in one place, back together and with things the way they were."

"Things will never be the same, they always change. Even *you* are different, Kado."

He understood her meaning. *Mother is gone, Father may be dead, and Briaca...* His sister needed him. Lars still held her captive and she might soon be sold as a slave or worse. "We have to hurry," the boy decided. "We've no time to waste."

Both boy and aerouant rose to their feet. Kado eyed the creature closely, wondering if it had grown larger while they talked. She lumbered toward the waterfall and the opening it hid, looking back only once. In her glowing eyes he sensed a mixture of sadness and pride for her bonded one. That look gave him hope, a bit of optimism in which to find a little more courage.

Scooping up his satchel, Kado followed.

Chapter Sixteen

The aerouant led the way, keeping to the riverbank with snout to the ground. She worked like a bloodhound, with remarkable senses that led her vinculum onward. Despite her keenness, she lost the scent several times and the pair had to double back. Their trek stretched morning into afternoon and afternoon into evening.

"If we don't find them soon," she warned with heavy worry in her voice, "we will have to camp in the open."

Kado, remembering his first encounter with the voltur, shuddered. "How far away do you think they are?" he asked.

"Not very, but something is wrong. I feel like we've gone in circles. I can smell them all around, but only faintly."

"Perhaps they've gone," the boy suggested with a shrug. She responded with a grunt. Kado watched the dragon with interest. She had definitely grown, now the size of Father's prize bull. "Do you have a name?" he asked her.

"Yes," she replied flatly. Her tone made it obvious she intended to keep it secret.

"May I know it?" he begged.

"Eventually." She turned, heading away from the river toward a dense rock formation. "This way," she called, nearly running toward the structure.

"Why can't I know it *now*?" he begged. "If we're bound, *shouldn't* I know it?" He made a reasonable argument, but she only moved faster. Kado had to sprint to keep up.

What at first appeared to be rocks were stone monuments, obelisks from another time erected by people long gone from the earth. Several held carved inscriptions and the aerouant frowned at the runes.

"*Thoir an aire do na h-uile a ta ciontachadh,*" she read. "Beware all who trespass."

"Did the voltur leave that as a warning?" Kado asked.

"I think not." Her fiery eyes swirled with mystery as she considered the possibilities. "I did not expect to find something like this, not here."

"Why not?"

"This predates the people of this land, back to a time of the Ancient Ones."

"Ancient Ones..." Kado considered her words. "You called Argant that, and so did the elder dragons."

"Then I chose the wrong description just now. The people who built these monuments lived when he was already ancient," she answered distractedly. The aerouant puffed out a held breath, sending dust and debris flying from the base of the worn obelisk. She focused on a freshly revealed line of runic text.

Kado heard but did not understand. Perhaps he had heard wrong. "How old *is* Argant?" he demanded.

"*Fon talamh tha deamhain,*" she read. "Beneath the earth lies demons." Without warning she reared, took a deep breath, and breathed fire out upon the flora entangling and hiding the stones.

Kado scrambled backward, away from the searing heat. He covered his eyes with his arms, an instinctive move he hoped the aerouant would not mistake for cowardice. When he again opened them, a world of wonder waited underground. The stones were ruins, the entrance to a tomb or temple beneath the forest floor.

With a mighty heave the aerouant pressed her shoulder against the opening, pushing the heavy stone aside. No dust fell, a sign the door was used recently and possibly often.

"They're strong, the voltur," Kado pointed out. "They could easily move that stone in and out of place."

"Yes," she agreed, "and I believe we've found their legion." She briefly glanced upward at the waning sun. If an aerouant could frown, she most definitely did. "We have to hurry."

"Wait!" Kado urged, pulling the dragon's tooth from his satchel and clutching it like a weapon. He was ready to go inside but needed more understanding. For that he wanted answers. "First tell me why you call Argant the Ancient One."

"Later," she growled in reply, anxious to finish the deed before nightfall. She pushed forward, squeezing between the open stones.

"Now, and also tell me your name!"

She paused, pulling back and spinning around to face the boy. Those eyes, swimming with fire, were not angry but spoke caution without words as she considered her answers. Finally, after several beats of Kado's heart, she let out a steamy sigh.

"My name is not mine to tell you, it is for you to figure out on your own. That is the final seal of our vinculum. As for Argant, his secret is *his* to tell whether you figure it out on your own or not. Respect these truths as the way it must be, Kado, son of Conrad and Oksana!"

The boy wavered, suddenly aware of how childish his demands had been. "I'm sorry," he said, begging forgiveness. "I understand."

"Thank you, now let's do this rotten business and get it over with." Letting out a grunt, she pressed through the opening and disappeared into the darkness.

With so many thoughts swirling in Kado's mind, he followed, keeping close to the aerouant while avoiding the back and forth swish of her mighty tail.

Chapter Seventeen

The structure was indeed a tomb, older and stranger than any Kado had ever seen. In his home village of Cardac, the dead were buried directly in the ground, it being soft enough to dig. But here someone had dug deep, so deep they reached a system of caves and tunnels into which burial rooms were carved. Thousands of human skulls and bones adorned every wall. The boy and the aerouant were especially careful not to disturb these remains.

Without torchlight, the aerouant lit the way with steady streams of fire from her nostrils.

"What are we looking for?" the boy asked the creature.

"Be quiet," she admonished. "Our enemy sleeps."

In one of the chambers Kado found an open sarcophagus, hewn from stone with the lid forced to the side. In it rested a voltur, its gaunt skin pulled tight across broad bones, with ghastly fangs protruding from its closed lips. Though it appeared dead, it breathed foulness into the air.

The aerouant stood in the tunnel and waited. "Go on, then" she said, realizing Kado needed prompting. He raised the dragon tooth into the air and brought it down, piercing the heart of the monster. Its life escaped with a single breath, bloodshot eyes opening wide with surprise.

The next few rooms offered the same ghastly experience. After vanquishing at least five more, killing sleeping voltur had become a mere ritual. Kado soon grew numb to it, no longer afraid but still sickened by the crunching of bone and splitting of leathery skin. Each time he brought down the tooth he breathed in a little more foulness, no matter how hard he tried to hold his breath.

At least there was very little blood, except once, when Kado grew lazy.

Having killed dozens, he carelessly missed the heart of one, hitting low and at an angle, rupturing the creature's stomach instead. The creature came awake immediately, ripping and clawing at the boy's neck, trying desperately for a last meal. The contents of its stomach, being blood and bile, spewed forth like a fountain, spraying all over the boy. Oh, how it reeked, the foul deadness of it all, the metallic and grim wrongness of evil.

Kado tried to get traction on the wet, stone floor, but could not. The voltur, though groggy and slow from recent awakening, slipped and slid with Kado in a life and death wrestling match, neither able to find footing. The boy was finally tossed aside and the aerouant had to move in and finish the kill, biting the foul creature's head clean off its body.

Kado nearly vomited when he heard the audible gulp of her swallow. Her irritated expression said all he needed to know about how *she* felt about such a meal. She belched the foulness into the room and shuddered, gagging but holding it down.

"I'm sorry," the boy offered.

"No matter," she replied. "I knew I would have to devour some eventually, I just wasn't prepared for how quickly their poison works within my body."

Kado felt compassion for the creature, placing a hand against her side. "Is there anything I can do?"

"No, I have organs that will filter it out, keeping theirs and my sanguis separate. It will pass through my body eventually, unless I choose to use it another way. Come," she urged, "the final room awaits."

Unfortunately, they reached that last room a bit too late. Row after row of sarcophagus filled it, each containing a voltur. There were dozens, many more than they could kill before some awakened. The sun over the forest above must have dipped far enough down that these had already begun that process.

Kado and the aerouant exchanged a look then sprang into action. What they had hoped would be a deliberate and controlled execution had turned into a cacophony of sloppy and violent slaughter. Each dealt death in what became a hellish scene of shouts, grunts, and dragon fire. It spewed forth like a strobe light, confusing and confounding the awakening enemy with its flickering and brilliant explosions.

The boy, no longer slowed by inexperience, moved fearlessly, driven by urgency and furiously stabbing voltur as quickly as he could before they roused from their coffins. The dragon roared angrily as she ripped hers into pieces with sharp teeth, gulping them down her gullet. All odds were in their favor until Kado lost his balance.

Four of the creatures, now fully awake and having reached full strength, immediately overwhelmed the boy. They tossed him to the ground, sending the dragon's tooth sliding away between a sarcophagus and the far wall. No matter how far he stretched he could not reach it, and gaunt hands held him down while sharp teeth reached for his throat.

A flashing tail swept all four, sending them flying in every direction. The aerouant, true to her word as his protector, moved like a serpent. Her long body quickly coiled, then struck out blindingly fast. She cut down two voltur with a single snap of the jaw and caught the other two with her talons, piercing their hearts with sharp claws. After she had finished, and the room no longer crawled with escaping vermin, her fiery eye surveyed Kado's skin for wounds.

"Kado are you okay?" she asked in a panicked voice, so out of character with her usual calm. After he was slow to answer she grew frantic with worry. "I'm sorry," she sputtered, "are you bit? Were you harmed by my careless fire? Oh, Kado, I would never forgive myself if you are harmed because I left your side!"

The boy eyed his dragon, recognizing something in both her voice and tone. The familiarity was one he could not place, but it felt nice to be cared for and watched over—something he had missed since Mother and Father had gone and left Briaca in charge. His sister was never as doting as either of their parents had been.

"I'm… fine," he managed, scrambling to his feet. He knelt to retrieve his dragon's tooth while she lit the room and checked for survivors. Bodies lay strewn all around, some already shriveled and beginning to rot.

"Kado," the aerouant beckoned with her voice, a bit nasally over the glowing flame from her nostrils, "look here." She stood before a monument, a stone sarcophagus with the visage of a man carved on the stone lid. "This must be him," she suggested. "The vampure they follow!"

The boy crossed the room, his eyes large with fearful recognition as his mind reasoned out the face. This was one he would never forget.

The dragon noticed his eyes and how his posture had changed. "What's wrong?" she asked. "Do you know this man?"

"Yes," the boy replied with sickness in his stomach and eyes that refused to leave the carving. "It is Lars, the man who has my sister."

The aerouant let out a fearsome roar filled with unbridled anger, the likes of which Kado had never witnessed. That roar turned into a scream that shook the walls. "Briaca!" she bellowed mournfully, her voice echoing through the chamber. The creature reared back, slamming her mighty head against the stone lid, cracking and sending crumbling pieces flying throughout the room. Inside the sarcophagus, instead of finding either corpse or revenant, she found only dust.

Turning, the aerouant led the charge from the tomb, racing through a maze of tunnels toward the moonlight waiting above. Kado raced after, chasing his protector and praying to his gods they would reach his sister in time. Both boy and beast had realized Briaca may already be taken, her body drained and turned into something else entirely.

Together they reached the entrance and Kado slowed. The aerouant was now too large to fit through the stones framing the opening. Without breaking her stride, she burst through them, crashing into the forest and sending a cloud of dust and debris that sparkled in the moonlight, falling like twinkling snowflakes as it settled beneath the trees.

"Hurry," she commanded, her voice sounding a lot like Briaca's with its newfound authority. "We have little time! Climb upon my back and become a dragon rider." The aerouant pressed her body low against the ground and spread broad wings, each spanning five paces wide. She was now at least twice that long, snaking toward the entrance as Kado emerged from the tomb.

When had she grown so powerful and big? he wondered.

What they had just accomplished suddenly became real to the boy, his mind returned to the bravery both had demonstrated beneath the surface. Slaying the undead was one thing, a legendary feat for a mere boy with or without an aerouant. That they had done it without ever considering running out, had committed their minds and bodies to the task no matter the outcome, had caused them both to grow.

He quickly pushed those prideful thoughts aside. Who was he to perform such heroics?

Scrambling up her tail and onto her back, he gripped two horns protruding from the aerouant's scapula. He wedged his feet between her scales and held on tight with his body.

"Are you ready?" she asked gently, as if worried he might fall off during flight.

"Fly, Mother," he begged, and Oksana beat her wings with a vengeance, lifting high above the treetops and soaring higher than the clouds. Cardac, and Briaca, depended upon their arrival.

Chapter Eighteen

Flying so high, so fast, filled Kado with a rush of excitement. As the wind blew past he realized he no longer feared heights, at least not atop Mother's back. After all he had endured, balancing on the cliffside not just once but twice, he calmly felt at home in the sky. Her presence settled that sense of maternal longing he had missed for so long. He finally felt safe, cared for, and loved. He also marveled at the irony that his mother was a dragon.

"How did you know?" she asked, her voice that of an aerouant but finally recognizable as Oksana's.

"It was your love, the way you reacted when you thought I might be injured. Before you left, you were always there when I hurt myself, looking me over just the same way. Also, you knew about Briaca, even though I never told you her name."

"I told you it was your job to figure out who I was and you did it, just like I knew you would," she praised him.

Finally, Kado understood their bond and her growth. When he began this journey, he was driven more by anger than courage but now felt different. Her love, her *presence* explained so much. "So courage alone isn't what makes an aerouant grow?" he asked.

"Yes, it helps, but isn't everything. The aerouant grows depending on the vinculum bond, which itself depends on how deeply aligned the aerouant and human's needs match up. You were alone, your entire family gone, and I was lonely. We both *needed* the bond. I needed my children and you both needed me. Briaca still does. It panged me to remain silent. I was forbidden from revealing my identity until you figured it out. We never would have fully bonded had you not."

"Why did you leave us in the first place, Mother? Had you stayed we wouldn't have needed the vinculum."

"I had to leave because I have always been dragonkind. Our first form resembles humans so closely not even a vampure can tell us apart without thorough inspection. I was sent away from my thunder, my first family, out of duty. I was destined to become an aerouant, a protector of innocence and wisdom, but first had to contribute to a bloodline through which dragon walkers could emerge. You too are dragonkind, blood of my blood, Kado, and so is Briaca."

The realization felt so odd. *Dragonkind.* The boy scarcely understood its meaning, but his imagination would soon run away with possibilities. "But why did you leave? Didn't you love Father?" he asked solemnly.

"With all my heart."

"And us? Didn't you love Briaca and me?"

"Of course I did. That's why it hurt so badly to leave, but I had to go. I was only given a short time in human form, long enough to give birth and then leave, but I stayed longer than I should have. I wanted to raise both of you as long as I could."

"That's why you told us the story of Erwan the Bold," Kado realized. "You wanted to ensure that, when one of us needed you the most, we would seek an aerouant and find you."

"Yes, but I honestly doubted I would ever see you again and hoped that whoever did come to bond was at least one of our lineage."

"So, as I found my courage, it made you grow?"

"You already had courage but were filled with doubt and lacked strength. I had strength but needed love. What made me grow was your trust in dragonkind, both in me as your protector and mother, but also in yourself."

"Mother," he asked as they started their descent, the tiny fires of Cardac flickering below, "who is Argant the Storyteller? Is he Erwan the Bold?"

"I already told you that secret is *his* to tell."

"But he *is* dragonkind, isn't he? I'm certain of it. I've seen his staff; it's made of dragon bone. I've also seen his aerouant, it's a skeleton now. It died, didn't it? Argant outlived it?"

Oksana let out a deep sigh but kept the old man's secret. "Ask him for the truth the next time you see him, and perhaps he will tell you."

Kado opened his mouth to speak just as she dove, and his words of protest trailed off behind them. As the ground rushed up, he scanned the village for Lars and his thugs.

From out of nowhere, a dark shape crashed into the side of Oksana, folding her right wing and sending them into a sideways spin. They were falling without any way to recover flight. The longhouse loomed directly beneath them, and they would certainly crash through its roof.

"Hold on tight, Kado!" the dragon cried out to her rider, fighting against the spin and turning her body to protect her son from the impact. She absorbed most of the blow as they tore through the thatch roof and landed hard on the feasting table below. Its legs blew apart as the tabletop splintered beneath Oksana's weight.

The boy tumbled off and rolled. He felt two ribs crack as they struck a wooden beam.

With lights of pain flashing in his eyes, he looked up at his aerouant mother. She had regained her feet, standing to face off armed men rushing to attack. They had been ready for her arrival and had set a well-laid trap.

Oksana's long body whipped and thrashed as they stabbed and slashed with spears and swords, forcing her backward into the fireplace, scattering its embers and bellowing ash. They moved with blinding speed. Kado realized these were not men, they weren't even voltur, these fought with the strength of lesser vampure. One of them pricked a scale, tearing it off and revealing pink tissue beneath.

"There!" one of the soldiers shouted. "It has a wound, attack it there!"

Oksana did her best to protect her weakened armor, turning her body and absorbing their blows with her back.

"No!" Kado cried out. Despite his newfound courage, he was untrained, unable to fight these larger men. He reached into his satchel for his blade, forgetting his pathetic little knife had shattered against the breast of a voltur. Instead he drew out the dragon's tooth, wondering if it would work as well on vampure as it had the lesser creatures.

A dark shape descended into the hall, dressed all in black and with leathery wings, its pointed fangs hung low against a bloody bottom lip. Though it was not human there was no mistaking the vampure visage of Lars. Horns now protruded like a crown on his head. His eyes, swirling orbs of crimson, locked on the boy, his claw-like finger outstretched and pointing him out. "Stop him," he commanded his minions, "before he summons the others!"

These words confused Kado, but then he understood. Lars had seen him holding the horn. Despite the pain of breathing in, his broken ribs protesting as air filled his lungs, he placed the dragon's tooth to his lips and blew, sounding the alarm and calling all dragonkind in the area.

Stars formed in his eyesight preventing him from seeing one of Lars' thugs approach. The man ripped the tooth from the boy's hands, and Kado felt a heavy boot hit hard against his ribs. The room swam from the pain as he struggled to hold onto consciousness.

The door to the longhouse opened and three more soldiers rushed in. With pikes held aloft they rushed forward, shoulder to shoulder to face the dragon. "We saw the thing plummet and are here to help!" one of them cried out to those fighting.

Through foggy eyes Kado watched them, slowly recognizing one. "Father!" he called.

Conrad's scarred face turned toward his son's voice. His eyes grew wide with recognition, and he called out again, "Don't worry, we'll save you, son! We saw the dragon attack as we approached the village. Go, now! Run for safety while we help kill it!"

"No! The dragon is *good*, Father! He pointed a finger at Lars, whose wicked fangs smiled back at the boy. "*This* vampure kidnapped Briaca! He has her hidden away!"

"Kado is right! Kill the vampure, Conrad!" the aerouant urged the pikeman.

Confused by the dragon's ability to speak, all three pikemen froze in place, looking between the dragon and the vampure. Conrad especially found himself distracted, detecting a hint of his wife's voice in its speech. He blinked uncertainty, his features basking in the moonlight flooding through the open ceiling.

Kado looked upon his father's expression and felt sadness. The man did not yet understand this dragon was his wife and needed more time to piece it all together. Climbing to his feet, the boy inched closer to the thug now holding the dragon's tooth. Without turning to face the warlord he called, "I blew the horn, Lars! What will you do after more dragons arrive, more against whom you can defend?"

"It's too late," Lars explained. "I've already summoned my own legion!"

Kado laughed despite the pain stabbing his ribcage. "Mother and I killed your brood! All of them, each of your voltur are dead. We found them asleep in the tomb beneath the ruins!"

"Lies!" It was Lars' turn to laugh and turned to watch his soldiers surround the aerouant, keeping her pinned down by their swords. The soldier beside Kado gripped the horn, also caught up in watching the dragon.

"I am *not* lying! Mother and I found them, hidden beneath ancient ruins. *Fon talamh tha deamhain*," he added. "Beneath the earth lies demons, Lars! And we found them! Mother and I *killed* your legion of demons!"

His words had the intended effect, both on Lars and also his father. The vampure grew angry, but not enough to turn away from the dragon.

Conrad began putting the pieces together. "Mother?" he muttered, thinking of the stories his wife had told the children, of dragons and their bonded riders. He watched his son with confused silence, and silently mouthed the word again. "Son, your mother left us. She is not here."

"Conrad, help me against these soldiers," the aerouant begged. "We must protect Kado and find Briaca."

The pikeman finally recognized his wife's voice despite its rumbling tone. He nodded to his partners and they reluctantly agreed, stepping beside the dragon and pushing back the swordsmen taking her on.

While all eyes watched the scuffle, they missed seeing Kado making his move. The thug beside him still gripped the tooth and turned too late, unable to stop the boy from drawing a long dagger from his belt. He let out a gasp as it entered his body, rammed upward beneath his ribs and quickly finding the heart. The dragon's tooth tumbled from dying hands and landed on the floor.

Kado knelt, grabbing the relic and holding it aloft. The bloodstains from the many voltur he had slain shown crimson in the moon and firelight. "Look upon this tooth, Lars," the boy commanded. "We found your tomb, smashed your sarcophagus, and killed every last one of your demons! Your brood *is* dead, and so soon shall *you* be."

Lars turned, his eyes wide with anger, and charged with incredible speed. He flew across the room with wings beating fast and arms outstretched.

Kado did not budge, holding the dagger with his right hand and the dragon's tooth in his left. Without flinching he faced his attacker's rampage. Though he did not know what to do, and was too terrified to try anything but stand there, he drew strength knowing his mother would protect him.

Across the room Oksana swung her tail over the heads of the pikemen, sending an eruption of embers into the air as she swept the fire and struck the soldiers square across their chests. They flung against the far wall, striking with a sickening crunch of broken bone. From the corner of his eye Kado watched his mother move with lightning quickness, knocking Lars away from her son, his fangs mere inches from her son's neck and about to strike.

Lars rolled into a heap of leathery wings, his breath knocked free and his mind stunned from the blow. The vampure lay there twisted, beaten by the aerouant looming over his mangled body.

Conrad rushed to his son's side while his pikeman friends flanked the dragon, pointed their weapons at the vampure she held pinned. "Kado, are you okay?" he asked, nearly shaking the boy. "What is going on?"

"I'm fine," Kado told his father, wrapping him in a tight embrace. "But Briaca is missing. This... *thing* took her." He smiled. "But I found *Mother* on Mount Sapientia and brought her back to help us."

Conrad turned, looking upon his wife—no longer a woman but now a snarling dragon standing over a fallen vampure. "Oksana, is it really you?" he asked.

"It is I, Conrad," the aerouant spoke, her fiery eyes dimmed by sadness. "I'm sorry I could not tell you before, but I had no choice but to leave and now you know why."

"I no longer care about why," the boy's father said with a laugh, staring up at the beast. "I only wish I understood *how*."

"I have always been dragonkind," she told him. "My bloodline descended from the Ancient One himself. I'm sorry I could not tell you. I was sworn to secrecy."

"Why?" Conrad asked, his mind suddenly racing with so many questions.

"It was for our children," she answered. "That is all I can say. I will tell you more, if there is time, but for now I must rid the world of this plague." She leaned low over Lars, cringing as if preparing to eat a rotten morsel.

Lying in her shadow, Lars managed enough strength to raise his head off the ground. One of his injured fangs sat crooked in his smile as he said, "You fools. Dragon horns don't only call dragonkind. They also call vampure, letting them know it's time to dine!" He raised a single, dark claw and pointed at the broken ceiling.

A dark shape fluttered above the opening, cautiously waiting and watching the chaos below. One by one other figures joined the first, lowering themselves into the lodge with leathery wings. There were six vampure in all. Two lunged at the pikemen and two attacked Oksana, biting and tearing at her scales. The others helped Lars to his feet and moved into a defensive position in front of him.

All of these newcomers wore the clothing of nobles.

The aerouant thrashed against her attackers, biting and beating them back with her head and tail. But these vampure fought with more speed and greater strength than the others, being advanced in form and far more experienced in fighting dragons.

Conrad and his partners locked their bodies together and pushed back their attackers. As dragon fire flashed, he recognized one of the vampure, the one lunging for Oksana. "Lord Eduard!" he exclaimed.

The nobleman for whom he had fought a long and drawn out war had latched onto the dragon, his sharp teeth biting frantically at her missing scale. "Kill them all," he commanded the others between bites, "then quench your thirst with dragon blood!"

The pikeman gave his own attacker a swift punch to the jaw with the handle of his weapon, spinning and handing him off to his partners. They turned him and the second vampure with a coordinated step, freeing Conrad to attack Lord Eduard.

He ran, intent on protecting the aerouant, swinging the long pole downward against the nobleman's back. The tip of his weapon shattered and the vampure turned and hissed but returned its attention to the dragon. This human was no threat. Rearing back, he struck, plunging white fangs deep into her soft underbelly. His body shook with pleasure as he slowly consumed her lifeforce. Try as he may, Conrad could not dislodge the vampure, now devouring sanguis from the aerouant beneath his futile punches and kicks.

From across the room, a door opened and another form arrived. A young woman, dressed in simple clothing, stepped into the hall. She was tall, with flowing dark hair.

Kado recognized his sister at once. "Briaca!" he cried, causing Oksana and Conrad to look away from Lord Eduard. As the girl stepped into the firelight, they all noticed her face lacked luster, dun and drained as if she had already transformed into one of the vile creatures. On her neck and chest were bite marks, revealing several days of Lars' unbridled feasting.

Chapter Nineteen

Kado watched his sister's arrival, filled with sadness and shock. They had arrived too late. She stood in the warm firelight, unfeeling of its warmth. Though she stared in her brother's direction, she did not see him, looking past or through. He could only imagine what she had endured in such a few days. What he noticed most about Briaca were her eyes, swirling pools of bloody crimson with no white to them at all.

"Would you like to feast?" Lars asked, stepping out from behind his protectors, as casually as if offering a walk in the garden. As he wrapped his arms and body around Briaca, his claw-like fingers, so grotesque in this vampure form, caressed her neckline. He stroked the punctures he had left, admiring how no scab had raised on any of them, then ran his tongue across each, tasting his handiwork. Her skin glistened with the remains of his wet saliva.

As if aroused by his touch, Briaca's mouth instantly watered, a bit of drool sliding down her chin. She licked her tongue across pale lips, revealing fangs had emerged where normal teeth had previously been. She turned away from Kado, her eyes yearning for dragon's blood, and watched a stream of it flow down Lord Eduard's chin.

Oksana still struggled, though her strength had noticeably faded. Her fiery eyes had dimmed and weakly watched her daughter's sad display of bloodlust.

Get up, Mother! Kado begged in his mind, hoping the aerouant would find strength to stand and fight.

Conrad's fellow pikemen abruptly backed away, filled with terror as their two opponents overpowered and broke the long weapons in half. The men appeared ready to flee into the night, but their feet remained fixed by fear. All at once Lar's companions joined the others, sprinting across the room to feed upon those defenseless soldiers. The four noble vampure fell upon them, biting and chewing their lives into submission. Meanwhile, Eduard sucked the life from Oksana.

Now Kado and his father stood alone facing the warlord and an entranced Briaca, focused on reasoning with whatever part of the girl remained. They watched helplessly as the girl slowly approached.

"Briaca, honey, it's me," Conrad reminded his daughter. "I'm back from the war," he told her. "I'm home again and we're together."

But all recognition had disappeared from her eyes, and those swirling pools of blood seemed only to reflect a stranger. Her abrupt, inhuman movement became faster than a voltur, faster even then Lars and the other vampure, as she leapt upon her own father to feast.

Kado recoiled, stepping away as his sister knocked Father to the ground.

From across the room, Oksana groaned, her fading eyes now paled to a soft yellow. They turned to watch her daughter drain her husband. In that moment the dragon found enough strength to swing her massive tail, hitting Lord Eduard and sweeping the other vampure off the pikemen. They landed hard against the logs walling the lodge, their impact cracking the wood and allowing bits of moonlight to trickle inside. All six stood up at once, leaping on the aerouant with renewed thirst, using their claws to rip away scales. Their fangs reached the soft, tender flesh beneath.

Kado watched, frozen by fear, unmoving and unable to help either Mother or Father. He watched, horrified, as his sister feasted on human sanguis.

Blood of my blood, their mother had earlier explained.

Briaca should not be changed, he reasoned. *She isn't human, how could she transform into vampure?*

Then he realized she wasn't like Lars. His sister had transformed into something worse, far more sinister and much more dangerous than vampure. Both Oksana's children were dragonkind, and Lars must have realized that when he devoured Briaca's sanguis, why he had chosen to turn her instead of sold her off like the others. His and her sanguis had combined, mixing and creating something foul. What devoured their father terrified Kado, causing him to tremble to his very core. Conrad's lifeforce sprayed across the hybrid's pallid cheeks but she failed to notice, too focused on consuming her meal.

Looking away toward his mother, Kado watched Lord Eduard and the others. Like leeches they clung as she feebly writhed, dying and unable to fight them off. Standing helpless and alone as his parents perished, he watched his sister move closer to damnation. Kado ripped his attention to face Lars.

"She's special," the warlord said with a shrug, meaning Briaca. He licked his lips as if tasting her from afar. "I just didn't know *how* special she was when I found her. No, that revelation came after I first tasted her sanguis. I have tasted dragon's blood before, but never untainted. They always poison their blood when they know they will be feasted upon, rendering us ill and weakening the effects of the sanguis. She, like you, did not know your mother's lineage."

"You've turned her into a monster," Kado accused, "a hybrid you did not intend."

"Perhaps," the warlord said dismissively, smiling as Conrad heaved a final sigh then fell lifeless. "But she empowered me more than I strengthened her. Such a sweet gift she has given through her ignorance, one I believe you will also share with me."

Briaca finished draining her father and looked up from her meal. Her bloody eyes fixed on Kado. She and her master leapt in unison toward the boy, moving too fast for him to fight either off. On each side of his neck the bites came, followed by the thirsty slurping of ravenous hunger.

Poison them, he told himself, *like mother surely will!* But, like his sister, he did not know how. Lars and Briaca would take on a greater form of vampure if he could not figure out how, but his thoughts blurred and the boy quickly forgot why he should even bother trying.

An odd sensation of contentment flooded the boy, a guilty sense of joy in giving over what these two so desperately needed. Kado ceased struggling and gave his lifeforce willingly.

These vampure *had* to consume him. He would not deny them the power they deserved. He gave all of himself, staring up at the hole in the ceiling.

His death would allow others to live.

As his vision darkened, the room grew strangely brighter. His mind had withdrawn. Moonlight flowed through this subconscious.

Isn't it wonderful? a voice spoke into his mind. *Give in to the thirst!*

Kado felt it, that wanton thirst. He wanted also to feed, and longingly turned his eyes toward Oksana, wondering if the feasting vampure would save any of her sanguis for him.

Yes, you want her, don't you?

Who are you? Kado asked the voice.

I am Goro, the Lord of Blood, and I will show you my story, how I was betrayed by the Keryx and the one you call the Ancient One.

Visions flashed as his own thoughts retreated. Where his mother had planted stories about the legendary dragon riders, new tales sprung forth of evils he had never imagined. Instead of heroes he suddenly knew the mythos of darkness, evil that walked the earth in search of endless feeding.

A shadow passed over the lodge, a large shape that seemed to stir new thoughts inside of Kado, strange ideas like beating his wings to fly off into the distance. The shape had been a dragon, even if he was slow to recognize his next meal, and he yearned to chase it down in flight.

"Enough!" a voice bellowed from the doorway. Abruptly the room fell into full darkness. One heartbeat. Two. Then the room exploded with strobing lights.

Every vampure in the room pulled away from their meals, drunk by their feasting and blinded by the sudden brilliance. Each of the creatures, once noble by birth and position, found themselves rendered wretched by the light. It stung their skin as they retreated. They covered their eyes behind leathery wings, each appearing sluggish and dazed from so much sanguis.

As Lars and Briaca released Kado, he blinked clarity, his trance less intoxicating without their saliva entering his wounds. Even Goro's voice trailed off into silence. The boy turned his head, partially aware of Argant the Old, the ancient storyteller, holding his dragon bone staff like a fairytale wizard. He stood in the doorway wearing a fierce scowl.

"Enough!" the old man said again.

Dregal, the massive aerouant abruptly arrived, tearing apart the wall beyond Oksana. He charged inside and chomped two vampure in a single bite. He quickly consumed their pieces while Lord Eduard and three others roared displeasure. The aerouant backed them off Oksana with a roar. All four vampure held their bellies, bloated and full and staggering with dizziness.

That's what Lars meant, Kado realized. *Mother tainted her blood! They stagger because they're poisoned like the voltur I first killed behind the waterfall.*

He raised his eyes toward Briaca and Lars. This pair suffered no weakness. After drinking the boy's pure sanguis, they seemed even stronger than before, especially Briaca.

The entire ceiling then ripped away. Through the gap emerged the skeletal remains of an ancient dragon, larger than two Dregals and at least four Oksanas. More than a dozen wyverns flew past this monstrosity, just as two full-sized Elderkin peered in with angry, swirling eyes. They had come to not only kill, but to feast upon vampure.

Fast and nimble this dragon army charged Lord Eduard. He tried to fight back but faltered, wracked by the pain in his bloated belly. Dregal moved in for another kill but Eduard drew a silver sword, plunging it deep into the fiery brightness of the dragon's eye.

The beast roared, his misery momentarily emboldening the drunken vampure.

He fought against the wyvern with renewed vigor, fierce but short lasting. Dregal recovered, knocking the sword from the nobleman's hand, sending it flying across the room. Two wyvern grabbed the vampure from behind and tightly held him before their protector. Dregal struck quickly, piercing Eduard's chest with a single swipe of his claw.

Argant, full of vigor, grabbed the doorframe with one hand, pushing it wider with inhuman strength. One by one the walls fell, the building itself falling apart. In mere moments, an entire thunder of dragonkind devoured the remaining vampure trapped within.

Kado watched as the frenzied creatures tore the vampure asunder with ferocious bloodletting. By the time they had consumed the final piece of vampure flesh, the dragons encircled both him and Briaca. With teeth bared, the beasts snarled and growled at the sickness festering within.

Dregal stepped over the wyvern and leaned in, sniffing Briaca's skin. "They're infected," he accused. "We should kill them now, Ancient One, and be done with your experiment!"

"Of course they're infected," Argant replied joyfully. "Just as I expected and hoped! I *told* you this was the way it had to be!" He looked around, scanning the room for someone or something. "In your fury, you let Lars escape," the old man pointed out. "*That* wasn't part of the *experiment*, as you called it. Go, find him. See if he leads you to Goro. He's tasted pure sanguis twice now and will be closer soon in form to his master!"

Dregal gave a huff and an angry roar, rising high into the sky before slowly circling the village.

Argant shoved his way inside the circle of dragons, using his staff to shoo them aside. All gave the storyteller room, all except the animated skeleton. It came closer, examining the children and tasting the air around them.

Kado stared upward, too intoxicated to protest.

"You'll become like your sister if you don't follow my instruction," Argant explained, his tone full of compassion and a bit of sympathy.

"Unless you do as I say, you will both be cursed by this infection, forever doomed to thirst. The eternal hunger will corrupt your soul and you will live out your days like the vampure."

In that moment Kado felt it, he already wanted to feed, *needed* to consume sanguis, and stared up at the old man wantonly. He could almost taste his nectar. Somehow this was no human but dragonkind.

"Bring them to *me*, Ancient One," a weak voice called out. It was Oksana who spoke, and Kado recognized his mother despite her aerouant form. She lay still and dying, drained of color as well as life. The cool breeze of night chilled his skin, raising up tiny bumps in the moonlight.

Part of the boy yearned to drink the rest of what she offered, but a small sliver of his existence wanted to run to her, to hug her neck and cry. *I cannot lose her again,* that part of him whispered, soothing that which hungered.

Brother and sister felt their arms squeeze tightly around their bodies, paralyzed by unseen magic that lifted both to their feet. Argant's staff nudged each from behind, coaxing them toward their mother's deathbed. She lay still upon the embers of what had once been a roaring flame of warmth.

Despite thirst was taking over, Kado managed to speak as Oksana's son. "I failed you, Mother, and also Father and Briaca."

"No. You have done well, my son. But now you have a choice. You may give in to the dragon thirst that drives the vampure, or choose to serve your bloodline. It's time, son, to choose your form, just as I chose mine."

"I don't understand."

"When you first found me atop Mount Sapientia, you believed the other aerouants and I to be young. Argant told you we were *not* young, and he told you the truth. We were small because we were unbonded. Dragonkind do have young, but not as you would expect. When we hatch from our eggs we have the same form as you, we appear human. Only after we mature and emerge from our first metamorphosis do we appear as dragonkind. I was young when

Argant asked me to go into the human world, where I met and fell in love with your father, bore him two human children who could adopt a different form altogether."

"None of this makes sense," Kado insisted again.

"You're dragonkind," Argant snapped, "but no longer like us. You're sanguis is mixed with that of the vampure, and it's time for you to choose your next form. You could emerge as mostly dragon, a hybrid who walks among humans with greater powers, or choose to serve Goro's dragon thirst and take the form of that dark lord. Be warned, his disease flows through your veins, and we must kill you if that is what you'd rather become."

To Kado's surprise, Briaca managed to speak. Her voice quivered like a toddler first balancing on their legs and sounded like she had not spoken for years. "I killed Father," she said, her words neither a statement nor question. She had only just realized her crime. "There's no hope for me."

"There *is* hope for you," Oksana assured her daughter. "The disease inside you killed Conrad. Just as villagers should not blame any traveler who brings a plague, you shall not be blamed for quenching that hunger before given your choice. True, you drank human sanguis, truer it was your father's, but you have a chance at redemption now after tasting the sanguis of your brother."

"How?" Kado asked. Part of him wanted to wrap his hands around his sister's neck, to strangle her for what she did to Father. Mother was wrong, there would not be any forgiveness nor redemption for doing such a thing. But another part of him felt intensely jealous, wishing it had been *him* who drained the pikeman of lifeforce. "I feel it in me too," he admitted, defeated. "How can redemption be possible?"

"By curing the illness," Argant explained. "Your sister has nearly broken free of its grip, but the disease still holds. There is one way to cleanse you both."

Kado wondered at the old man's words. Then he fully understood. "She drank my blood, tasted my sanguis, and that helped her find clarity."

Argant nodded. "You gave her the purity of your blood, and that cleared much of her confusion brought on by the plague. But it isn't enough. You are half human, and therefore your sanguis could not fully cleanse her, could not restore her as dragonkind. She needs something... purer."

Kado's eyes fell upon his mother, dying at the feet of her children. "I cannot," he said. "I can't kill my own mother."

"Nor can I," agreed Briaca.

"You won't have to," Oksana said sadly, "because you *cannot*. I already released my poison and tainted my blood for all who would drink of it. If you drank it now, it would destroy you like this same poison once killed Dominus Titus."

"Then how?" Kado asked, looking around. All the other dragonkind still watched, but seemed unwilling to make the sacrifice.

"I am Argant," the old man quietly explained, "called the Ancient One. The form you see is not my own, but of my vinculum, Erwan the Bold. He granted me this body so that I may once again walk among the humankind. I am a dragon walker, able to appear as human while still clinging to my elder form." The skeletal dragon shook, rattling bones and giving off a bit of flame from its nostrils.

"So you really are the original Lord of Fire?" Briaca asked, her voice filled with awe.

"Yes. I am the same."

"I saw that," Kado realized, "just a few minutes ago while Lars and Briaca..." he could not finish the sentence, refused to put into words what his sister had done.

"Yes," Argant agreed. "Goro's memories flow through you just as they did your sister. But you will also receive mine if you choose our form. Erwan did not bond an aerouant as in the stories I have passed down to cover the truth, nor did he bond a mere Elderkin. He boldly bonded the sire of all dragonkind then gave up his life so that the Lord of Fire would walk among men."

"Why?" the boy demanded. "Why would anyone make such a sacrifice?"

"Ask your mother," the old man said.

Kado opened his mouth to ask, but Briaca spoke instead. "Why, Mother?" she asked. "Why did you sacrifice yourself for us?"

"My mission among humans was to provide the conduits for this new form of dragonkind. Just as Argant is a dragon walker through Erwan's sacrifice, so may both of you gain dragon form through another's sacrifice. Once you have been redeemed you will change. That you have been tainted by the vampure will grant resistance to the disease that lives in vampure saliva. You will be cured, you will transform, and you will walk this earth with longevity, strength, and the wisdom of your ancestors."

"But you will still be dead," Kado protested, "and so will Father."

"You would have outlived us both nonetheless," Oksana said dismissively. Her strength had faded to the point she could barely talk. "I'm tired now and need to sleep. Make your choice, but remember you will have consequences either way you decide."

"I want redemption," Briaca said immediately. She did not need time to decide.

Kado wanted to reply just as quickly, but something bothered him deeply. Mother had sacrificed her life for her children, had allowed those vampure to drain her until Argant and the others could arrive. She now lay before him dying.

"Who?" the boy asked. "Mother's bond will transform me as her vinculum, but who else must give up their life so that Briaca may become one of these..." *Dragon walkers*, he said the word in his mind. It sounded foreign, even there. "Will it be Dregal? Because he doesn't seem to care for us at all!"

Argant met the boy's defiance with a somber smile. "You knew me as the storyteller, and so I shall tell you a tale. I shall speak to you of Argant the Ancient, the sire of dragonkind."

Chapter Twenty

Argant told his story without the aid of magic, lit by the moon high above and accompanied by the soft crackling of a dying fire. There was no need for theatrics, the graveness of the situation had built enough tension and expectation in everyone. The mood was set, and all eyes and ears focused on his tale.

"Goro," Argant repeated, "his name as ancient as mine. He, like I, was among the first Keryx conceived. Before us there were only two races, those heavenly beings sent to watch over mankind and the humans themselves. But species do not stay separated long, and soon their offspring became the substance of legends."

"The Romans called you Titans," Kado whispered. "Mother taught me that." He looked in Oksana's direction. So much of her strength had failed. He yearned to rush to her side, but his hands and feet remained bound by Argant's magic.

"Yes, and so did the Hellenes. The people of Judea call us Nephilim, and the Aryans had their own names. All of mankind remember the echoes of our existence, even if they have begun to forget our offspring."

Briaca looked to Kado and he nodded. They had both seen and experienced this part of the story. "You defeated Goro," she explained. "He fled the battlefield and hid underground but reemerged some-thing... *worse* than the vampure. Why *did* you turn on him? How did you know he couldn't be trusted?"

"I realized too late the plans of Goro, how he had instigated our cousins to start the Ancient War. *He* created that division, the distrust, the fear. Once we were at odds, we did the work for him, warring until weakened. After some had died and others had gone, disappearing into another realm, I called him out, though I could not prove what he had done. Thus we fought against each other. He fell upon me with his first legion, a mixture of voltur and vampure he had created in secret."

Telling this story saddened Argant, the painful memories difficult to tell. This was a legend few had ever heard, no human, certainly, and, by their expressions, only very few dragonkind.

"I thought I had defeated him, but I never found his body. While I reveled in the victor's celebration he, as you both have seen, descended into darkness to wait. While I took on a form of abundance and plenty, Goro transformed into one of eternal thirst and wanton damnation."

"You had no idea he was amassing another army?" Kado asked.

"His legions walked among the humans we looked down upon but never actually saw. It wasn't until I noticed our kind had dwindled over many eons, first losing friends, then family, and finally offspring," Argant lamented, "that I realized Goro was to blame."

"You had no warriors among you at that time?" Briaca inquired.

"No, mostly wyvern and drake. I was the only one wearing the form we now call Elderkin, which, as you see, is quite limited in movement. We took our time and developed the aerouant form, agile warriors who could best strike the vampure from the sky as well as endure most of their damage. I fought alongside these warriors, already battle-hardened and scarred myself, but my presence put our kind at significant risk if I were to fall. We nearly lost that second war as soon as it began, not anticipating Goro's warfare would include ambush and surprise. We lost so many scales and regrew just as many, yet we persevered. Eventually, we triumphed, earning a lasting peace for centuries and more."

Listening to Argant's tales, the boy measured the weariness lining the old man's voice. He was tired of many things, the greatest of which it seemed, was living.

"After the second war I settled down, took many spouses, and did my part to replenish our number. I allowed the greatest of our warriors to adopt the Elderkin form, the remains of which are those among us tonight."

He gestured weakly to the skeletal dragon now sleeping soundly beside Oksana. "What remains of me will soon be gone. I had no conception of time, nor how many more eon I would live. I had grown soft, my actions complacent, enjoying the lifestyle my children and grandchildren enjoyed. We were the apex predator, stewards of the earth responsibly harvesting its bounty at will. Very few took on the aerouant form—there was no need for protectors. But one day all that changed."

Kado found himself enraptured by the tale and noticed the other dragons appeared just as captivated. He realized his deep, aching thirst had noticeably subsided.

"But soon we noticed subtle signs that danger had returned to the world. Hunters failed to return home to the thunder and children disappeared while playing in the fields. These were dismissed as accidents or disregarded as chance. We could not conceive of the evil that had returned."

"Goro," Briaca whispered sadly.

Argant visible shuddered, deeply disturbed by the name. "Goro," he agreed solemnly.

"He's awful," she said, her hands trembling as they rubbed her arms against a chill. "The sensation I felt when he spoke... It was overbearing," she explained, "forcing me to relax and give myself over to Lars. He took me to a place in my mind and showed me stories, much like these you tell."

"And now he is coming again," Kado warned. "The voltur said so."

"Yes. He awakened during the time of Erwan the Bold. I sought him then, but he was hidden too well."

From high above, the sound of frantic flapping mixed with grunts of pain. All eyes looked upward to find Dregal had returned. His snakelike body reflected the moonlight, but several darker areas revealed scales had been ripped away by attackers. Some parts of his fleshy skin even bled.

"Did you find Lars?" Argant demanded.

"Lars fled eastward toward Dacia. I followed but was met by a horde of vampure. They swarmed me as I flew and, by the time I had fought enough of them off, I could no longer find Lars' scent. The sun is rising soon, so they allowed me to turn back. The Delta has disappeared and seeks his master."

"Goro," Argant again whispered quietly. "Lars will be elevated in his new form and will serve his dark master directly. With Lord Eduard's death, another will be chosen to fill his vacancy, and so on. If there are as many under the Evil One's command as you say, then our enemy has indeed grown strong enough to leave their shadows. We are weak and cannot fight a war, and so we must again go into hiding. We must hide away and transform our species one more time."

As if overwhelmed by the news, Oksana let out a final breath and died. Kado felt part of her rush into him, filling him with strength he had not expected. He had not expected the sensation, a quickening that pulsed his heart close to racing. All her memories rushed in at once, of her time among the thunder and also with humans. Those which brought her most joy had most certainly been shared with her husband and children.

All eyes turned toward her lifeless husk, then focused on Kado and Briaca.

"What do you choose, Briaca, daughter of Oksana?" Argant demanded. "Will you give in to the disease, joining forces with Goro, or choose to cleanse it through the blood of our kind?"

Tears filled her eyes just as remorse consumed her heart. "I want redemption," she said without hesitating. Argant's invisible force released her body at once, and she ran first to her father, dragging his body next to his wife. Kneeling beside the hot embers, she hugged them both and sobbed, quietly begging their forgiveness.

"And you, Kado the Courageous? Now that your mother's power has passed into you?"

"I choose transformation, to become a dragon walker and protector of our kind." Argant's magic dissipated and the boy ran to Briaca's side. He knelt, wrapping her shoulders with the soothing forgiveness she sought. Looking up at the storyteller he pleaded, "But please tell me who must make the sacrifice Briaca needs."

"To cleanse the vampure disease you must both consume pure dragon sanguis, the rarest and most ancient of all. For either of you to transform into what we need, you must consume what remains of *me*."

Kado nodded. He had already assumed as much.

"I will do it," Briaca said quietly.

"I will too," her brother promised. And thus Kado the Courageous and Briaca the Brave agreed to consume both Argant the Ancient and Erwan the Bold, joining the greatest legends in the history of dragonkind.

Chapter Twenty-One

The dragons conveyed Kado and Briaca far away from Goro's reach, flying them to a primitive, mostly uninhabited continent. Though mountains here were high, they were not near the grand, unscalable peaks the Romans had named the *Alpes*. A more suitable place was found, a deep cavern of strong granite with only bats to witness their metamorphosis.

Argant dismounted the skeletal remains of his former self, leading the children and his entire thunder underground. They would sleep for nearly two thousand years, perhaps a bit longer depending upon whatever bit of Oksana had been passed to the boy. Yes, Kado would be special, but how much so depended on their bond and how much his mother had given of herself before passing. That vinculum would strengthen the boy's senses but wouldn't fully emerge until long after eclosion.

"Here is suitable," the Ancient One said to all assembled. Turning to Dregal he added, "Guard the entrance to this cavern with your life, and do so until both have awakened. Our future depends upon their form."

The mighty aerouant nodded his agreement, making no argument against.

To Briaca and Kado, Argant said, "Your mother was not the only of my children to sire my lineage on this earth. After I took human form, and for nearly four hundred years, I spread my seed across the Roman Empire so that you will have allies in the future."

"How will we find them, your offspring?" Briaca asked.

"I will still be with you, rather my memories will remain. But your slumber will be a long one and the awakening will not be pleasant.

You will emerge from your chrysalis confused, blind, and afraid, but those feelings will pass. Eventually, that amnesia will fade, and you will share all the knowledge I have amassed over three hundred million years, dating to the arrival of our heavenly ancestors."

"How will we survive two thousand years" Kado wondered aloud, "without eating or drinking?"

"How does a caterpillar survive in its cocoon during metamorphosis? It has devoured so many nutrients by the time it forms the chrysalis, the larva needs no more. Its heart slows as the body changes, growing new tissues and organs for the new form. So, too, will yours."

Argant watched Briaca carefully. Her control over the vampure urges had already waned during their journey. If she were to avoid transforming into vampure, she would need to purge their poison with pure sanguis very soon. "There's no point dragging this out any further," he said. "The time for my death has arrived."

"How much of you will we need to drink?" Kado asked quietly, repulsed by the thought.

Briaca, on the other hand, seemed eager—too eager.

"You must drink until *all* of me is gone."

Kado touched his mouth, feeling the newly grown sharpness of fangs emerging. He appeared worried over much more than just the feeding, and stole a glance at his sister. He knew his sister might not choose the correct form.

Her eyes had finished their transformation and already reflected the blood of her thirst. Argant pitied her, but her pain and confusion would prove necessary. Had Erwan not slain his own children, they would have been the first hybrids instead of these. But he had, and it took the Ancient One four hundred years to prepare again for this moment. But these were stronger versions than he originally planned, Erwan's obstinacy had done him a favor after all.

Argant held out his wrists for the children. Their thirst needed no urging. The thunder looked away, repulsed by the sight, but the skeletal remains of the Ancient One curled around the trio as they feasted. The Lord of Fire watched with pride as his grandchildren consumed his sanguis, freely given and without poison. Only after his eyes became too weak to remain open did he allow them to close.

"Kado!" the woman's voice screamed into his ear. "Can you hear me?"

She sounded so familiar, this woman, and that name she kept calling also stirred memories.

"Damn it, brother! Shake loose of this quickly! We can't carry you and fight at the same time!"

The vehicle bounced and something heavy thumped against the roof. The man driving the horseless carriage spun his wheel, swerving and sending them off in a new direction.

"How long will he be like this?" the driver asked.

"I don't know!" the woman snapped. "Kado, can you hear me?"

Kado... that name again.

"He's burning up, like he has a fever," she observed.

"Did that happen to you?" the driver asked.

"No. My recollection wasn't anything like this at all."

Their voices faded off into the distance, a far off conversation both muted and muffled. All the man could hear was the cacophony playing out in his mind. It came as a rush of memories pouring forth all at once. Eventually, one became clearer than the others.

Beings from Heaven walked the earth, coupling with humans. Their children named themselves gods. As is the nature of man, they betrayed their fathers, clung to their mothers, and passed on bloodlines that merged with mortals. From these lines sprang forth magical beings, the sources of mythology that filled centuries of superstitious mankind with awe.

He watched a war fought by giants, huge beings thrashing and biting at their rivals instead of using weapons. Such constructs were of man, petty and beneath these Keryx. These Titans allowed primal instincts to decide their battles.

Two in particular came into focus, one with grand wings and four legs. This monster, the Lord of Fire, had a thunderous tail that whipped about and a massive body which absorbed his enemy's blows. He breathed flame against his foe walking on two legs, humanoid but gigantic, with leathery wings that resembled a bat's. With sharp fangs the Lord of Blood bit and snapped, intent on devouring his rival. Horns rose above the creature's head like a crown.

That image fled, replaced by another.

The time of Titans had moved on, ushering a new era in the world. Now their own spawn outnumbered the Keryx. One of these lines led him to view dragons. Another led him to something far more sinister.

"Vampure," the man whispered into the vehicle.

"Yes, Kado, and also voltur," the woman's voice answered back. The vehicle swerved again as it raced. "They're attacking us *now* and we need you to break this trance!"

Kado... The name finally settled as his own. "I am Kado."

"Yes," the woman replied.

"And you are Briaca."

"Bingo!" the driver hollered out. "Ding, ding, ding! Winner, winner, chicken dinner!"

Kado blinked his eyes, the visions faded but did not completely evaporate from his mind. "What is this vehicle?" he asked, running his hand along the strange interior.

The driver took his eyes off the road and grinned behind his large mustache. "A 1986 Bronco, the most badass SUV ever made. With a three-inch suspension lift, two inches of body, and..."

"Vince! Shut up and drive!" Briaca pointed a finger forward.

"How does it move without horses?" Kado asked.

"Oh, it's got plenty of horses under this hood, a 5.8 Windsor V8!" Vince replied, swerving to miss a dark object swooping down from the sky. No, not to miss but to hit it directly! The creature struck a heavy brush guard and disappeared beneath the vehicle. Both right wheels bounced over its body with resounding thuds.

"Vince, he *just* awoke. The first thing he learns about this century shouldn't be about cars!"

Vince shrugged. "Fine, I'll teach him about the culinary treats of our century. Let's shake these things and stop at Round Rock for some Whataburger. You like mustard, kid?" He swerved again, striking down two more voltur.

Kado stared up at his sister as more recent memories filled his head. "Where is Argant?" he demanded.

"He died so that we would transform. He's nothing more than bones now resting in the cave we just left."

"These memories, everything flashing behind my eyes, these are his?"

"Yes, his and all that were passed down to him."

"You've seen them too?"

"I have." Briaca had grown into a beautiful woman. She wore her auburn hair cropped short, showing off the same high cheekbones of their mother. She smiled down at her brother, no longer as irritable as before. Only her eyes had changed. The last time he had looked into them the whites had completely reddened. Now, reflecting the soft lights inside the vehicle, he saw the whites had returned, leaving behind two red circles where her irises had once been blue.

Kado shuddered at the reason they had changed. He reached up and touched her cheek, forcing a smile of his own. "You chose your form," he said softly, "as did I."

Tears trickled down her cheeks as she stifled a sob. She nodded. "We're fighting a war, brother. One we're currently losing."

"Is that why you awakened me early?"

"Yes. We need your help. Nearly all the dragons are gone."

"If they're gone, what are we fighting for?"

Briaca stole a glance at the human driving the vehicle. He hadn't swerved in some time, and seemed to have relaxed behind the wheel.

"We're fighting for humans now and for Argant's bloodline... *our* bloodline."

Kado sat up, taking everything in—Briaca, Vince, even their *Bronco* as he called it. The clothes they all wore had a peculiar strangeness. Simple and thin yet durable, smooth and almost silky despite strong. The trousers themselves gave him freedom to move around but seemed able to withstand the snags and wear of life.

He peered outside the window and watched the world blur past him. Except when flying with dragons, he had never imagined moving so fast as they did now. The face reflected in the glass was most certainly his own, but he was much older than he last remembered.

Kado's hair had grown long during his transformation and had also turned unmistakably blonde. It hung past his shoulders in long strands. What surprised him most was the beard, full and thickly covering his chin and neck.

He reached up and touched the glass. "I look like Father," Kado realized. He appeared to share the same age as Conrad when the man had died. The thought made him stiffen. He had almost forgotten those details. He reached upward, touching a spot on his own neck, the side his sister had bitten.

Briaca placed a hand on her brother's shoulder but pulled away instinctually. "It wasn't really me who did that," she tried to explain, but it was too soon, despite how many years had passed for her.

"I know it wasn't," he agreed, "yet it *was* at the same time. Are you like *them* now?" he asked. "Am I?"

"No."

"But your eyes are just like theirs."

"Only at night. It actually helps me walk among them when I choose, just as Argant promised."

The Ancient One had promised them many things if they accepted this form, had sworn they would become something quite remarkable. They would be dragon walkers, but the venom of the vampure still swam in their veins. Thankfully, the blood thirst had disappeared during Kado's transformation.

"And mine?" he asked, meaning his eyes. The reflective lights of the city had made it difficult to see the color of his own in the glass.

Briaca leaned forward, reaching over the seats, and grabbed a visor hanging above the passenger side. With a tug she ripped it free.

"Hey!" Vince protested. "I'm gonna need that! You know how ornery the sun is! It bounces around, teasing me while I drive!"

"Shush," she scolded the driver who went on muttering about how the angle of the sun would someday blindly run him off the road. She held up the visor, the center of which had a tiny mirror.

Kado saw clearly his own face. Yes, he had grown into the very visage of their father in all aspects but one. His eyes, burning like two pools of fire, swirled and danced like those of his mother the last time he saw her.

"You're him," Briaca said. "You are *the* dragon walker."

Loud popping sounds followed by a terrible shaking turned into an echoed thumping from the road.

"Both front tires have blown," Vince said in Gaulish but then cursed in that other language. The Bronco abruptly screeched and slowed momentum, swerving and squealing as it came to an abrupt stop. "Hey guys," Vince called to the others, pulling a black object from a compartment near his side, "we've got company."

Fifty voltur encircled the vehicle, closing in on it slowly.

"Are you ready?" Briaca asked her brother. "Have you the strength to fight?"

"I don't know how," Kado replied honestly. When he last walked the earth he had been a boy, courageous and bold but not a fighter. Though he had killed voltur, he had done so when they were asleep.

"Then stay in the car," Briaca said with a wink, "and I'll teach you later." She pulled a bundle of wrapped linen from under the seat and quickly uncovered the object within, a curved piece of ivory or bone.

No, not neither of those, Kado realized, recognizing the dragon's tooth he had once held.

Briaca and Vince threw open their doors and stepped out of the Bronco. Kado winced as both doors slammed shut once more.

Together the pair stood back to back, holding strange weapons in their right hands. Briaca also wielded the dragon's tooth with her left. She held it to her lips and blew a single, long note that echoed across the prairie. As she pulled it down she twirled it to face downward, ready for battle, smiling at the enemies rushing toward her.

The black weapons exploded into the night, flashing bright lights from tiny muzzles that resembled dragon fire. Kado watched with amazement as several voltur dropped before the fighters, thrown backward from some invisible impact. Both Briaca and Vince fired repeated volleys into the advancing horde, until the monsters came too close to range down. They quickly dropped the strange weapons and drew blades—short, dark swords that refused to reflect the moonlight above.

The fight that ensued blurred with inhuman speed as the voltur dashed around, biting and clawing at the pair. Though Briaca was noticeably faster than Vince, both out sped the creatures, striking out with overwhelming strength. The man used the hilt of his sword to land a blow across the chin of one attacker, sending it spinning away and crashing to the ground. With a single slice he brought down the blade, severing head from shoulders. The fight lasted only a few minutes before a heavy crash sent the Bronco bouncing on its suspension.

Kado watched as a large Elderkin and two wyverns rushed from their landings, ripping into the voltur and scattering them in every direction. A larger dragon appeared, one which seemed strangely familiar to the man. He had seen him before, long ago but in some other form. It scanned the battle with a single eye, the other coated over by a thick scale. With a gasp Kado realized Dregal was no longer an aerouant, he was an Elderkin and led the thunder raining down to join the fight. Five more wyvern flanked their master as three aerouants landed behind the retreating voltur. In a matter of minutes, none of the demons survived.

Kado fumbled with the door handle and pushed it open, stepping into the night. He ran straight for Dregal.

The massive beast turned, snapping at the man before cocking an angry head. He huffed two streams of fire, illuminating the battlefield and reflecting a grisly scene. A single, swirling pool of fire watched Kado approach.

Dregal snuffed the fire quickly out. "So you survived the transformation, it seems." It was more accusation than question.

"Yes," Kado agreed.

"Then it's time you stopped being a man and become the dragon inside of you." Dregal then turned toward Briaca. "Train him, teach him these new ways and make him ready. War is coming, and it's time we *all* came out of hiding to fight it."

The woman nodded. "I will, Ancient One."

Turning back toward Kado, Dregal added, "I was against this, what Argant proposed. But he was right. The time of our kind has passed, and this world belongs to man, now. It's too late for me, but our blended offspring will have a chance to share this world. We need those like Vincent who can walk among humans and live like them." He cocked his head toward Briaca and let out a rumbling growl of disapproval. "We also need abominations like you and your sister, it seems." With a great beating of wings, he rose into the sky, circled once, then headed off to their mountain home far in the west. His thunder followed.

Once they were alone, Kado eyed Vince carefully. The man appeared normal, no different than any other mortal. His head was bald and he wore a bushy mustache. He was fit for being middle aged, and Kado placed him somewhere in his forties. Other than his inhuman strength and lightning speed, there was nothing else out of the ordinary.

"Look closer, Kado," Briaca urged quietly. "Remember what you felt when we were in the caverns? When you sensed a vampure but none were about?"

"Yes, and I still sense that stain though all these are dead."

"You sensed *me* brother. We are both hybrids, but my form is more their kind than dragon. You bonded with Mother, and that kept your blood pure, protecting you from the virus Lars injected. That's why she died, Kado. Mother died saving *you* from this curse while Father's death strengthened this curse within me. Oh, brother, please forgive me."

Kado felt pain for his sister, a deep sadness that brought forth memories of Conrad and Oksana. He reached out, hugged her closely, and wept, finally mourning what they lost nearly two thousand years earlier. He also wept for his mother and her selfless sacrifice.

After a long embrace they pulled away and Briaca pointed toward Vince. "Look at him closely," she said. "See him with that feeling in your blood. Use that ability to examine this man, to see him with our bloodline instead of with your eyes."

Kado took a deep breath and closed his eyes, flipping through Argant's memories for any clue as to how that sense would work. Finally, after coming across the memory of an old man meeting a young child, he understood. Argant, as the storyteller, had sensed his grandchild before he even knew of his lineage. That was why he had taken special interest in the boy, and why he set all of this future into motion.

The dragon walker opened his eyes and saw the man before him with fresh clarity. Gone were Vince's human qualities. His eyes held the slightest bit of fire behind two dark irises. His skin, though outwardly human, was comprised of tiny scales interwoven and sprouting hair as if he were a mammal instead of reptilian. In his chest, a heartbeat warm blood. But the cold sanguis, that nectar of a dragon's soul, distinguished him from humans.

"Hi, cousin," Vince finally said with a smile to break the tension. He gave Kado a wink and holstered his black sword.

"Is that iron?" Kado asked, pointing at its hilt.

"Not entirely." Vince looked toward Briaca as if hoping she would explain. She did not, but rather walked a distance away in search of solitude. With a shrug he pointed toward the Bronco. "Come on," he said. "You also get to learn how to change a tire. The sun's going to be up soon, so those things won't return. But Austin's about forty miles away and I'm starving. Let's get these changed out so we can get home."

"I'll join you in a moment," Kado told the man.

Then he followed his sister, approaching the woman she had grown into but remembering a time, long ago, when a bossy teen had sent her little brother out into the rain for firewood. He yearned to run back to her then, to apologize for how he had argued, and to bring home a sled full of enough wood to warm their cottage for many weeks.

"We're not part of the thunder, are we?" he asked her.

"No, and we never will be. Not with Dregal in charge."

"Then I guess we're back to where we were before."

"What do you mean?" she asked, confused.

"We only have each other." He reached out and hugged her closely, squeezing his sister tightly, and silently vowing never to leave her alone again. No matter what danger tried to split them, or what crazy old man promised adventure, Kado and Briaca would never choose anyone or anything else over family.

Loved this tale?

Don't miss the story of Briaca!

Now read these events from her point of view. Experience more adventure while discovering Vampure Mythos!

Books by T.B. Phillips

Dragon Thirst
Legends (September 2023)
Mythos (September 2023)

Andalon Saga

Andalon Origins
Andalon Project (April 2022)
Andalon Paradox (April 2023)
Andalon Prophecies (Expected Winter 2023)

Dreamers of Andalon
Andalon Awakens (June 2019)
Andalon Arises (July 2020)
Andalon Attacks (December 2020)

Children of Andalon
Andalon Legacy (September 2022)

Corrupted Realms
Orphan Knight (July 2023)
Wailing Tempest (May 2021)
Howling Shadow (September 2021)

Chilling Tales
Ferryman (October 2022)

Corrupted Realms
Orphan Knight (July 2023)
Wailing Tempest (April 2021)
Howling Shadow (September 2021)